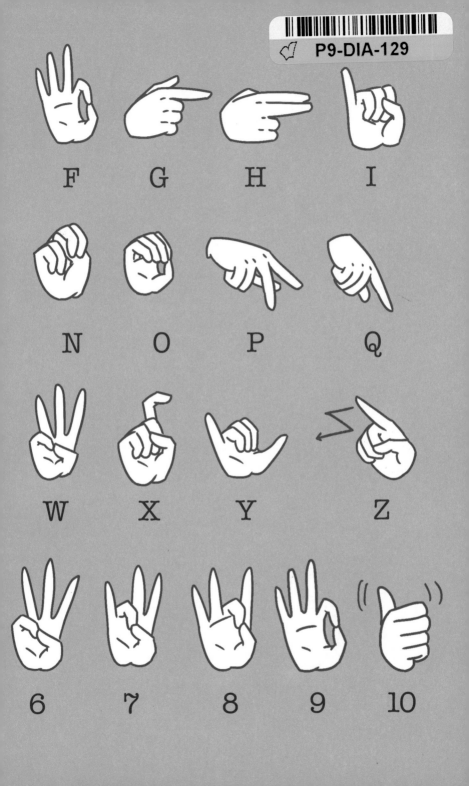

P9-DIA-129

Charlie & Frog

The Boney Hand

KAREN KANE

Disney • HYPERION

Text copyright © 2019 by Karen Kane
Interior illustrations copyright © 2019 by Carlisle Robinson

All rights reserved. Published by Disney • Hyperion, an imprint of Disney Book Group. No part of this book may be reproduced or transmitted in any form or by any means, electronic or mechanical, including photocopying, recording, or by any information storage and retrieval system, without written permission from the publisher. For information address Disney • Hyperion, 125 West End Avenue, New York, New York 10023.

First Edition, June 2019
1 3 5 7 9 10 8 6 4 2
FAC-020093-19109

Printed in the United States of America

This book is set in Adobe Caslon/Monotype
Designed by Marci Senders

Library of Congress Cataloging-in-Publication Data

 Names: Kane, Karen, author.
   Title: The Boney Hand : a mystery / Karen Kane.
   Description: First edition. • Los Angeles ; New York : Disney-Hyperion, 2019.
     • Series: Charlie & Frog • Summary: When a Castle-on-the-Hudson school
     legend suddenly goes missing, Charlie is the prime suspect, but he and his
     best friend, Frog, are determined to find the real culprit.
   Identifiers: LCCN 2018057156 (print) • LCCN 2018059833 (ebook) • ISBN
     9781368045865 (E-Book) • ISBN 9781368006286 (hardcover)
   Subjects: • CYAC: Mystery and detective stories. • Lost and found
     possessions—Fiction. • Theater—Fiction. • Schools—Fiction. •
     Deaf—Fiction. • People with disabilities—Fiction. •
     Grandparents—Fiction.
   Classification: LCC PZ7.1.K24 (ebook) • LCC PZ7.1.K24 Bon 2019 (print) • DDC
     [Fic]—dc23
   LC record available at https://lccn.loc.gov/2018057156

Reinforced binding

Visit www.DisneyBooks.com

SUSTAINABLE FORESTRY INITIATIVE   Certified Sourcing
www.sfiprogram.org
SFI-00993

THIS LABEL APPLIES TO TEXT STOCK

RICHMOND HILL PUBLIC LIBRARY
32972001936089 RH
The Boney Hand
Sep. 03, 2020

For Linda Flick and Jerry Levy, of blessed memory
and
for Glenn Hulse, our miracle man.

And for their family and friends who love them.

1. Cute

Myra and Alistair Tickler were trying not to be lousy parents. Really, they were. They were even reading books—parenting books—from the Castle-on-the-Hudson library. One book recommended something called quality time, which Mr. and Mrs. Tickler were spending right now with Charlie, who was wedged between them on the couch, as everyone waited for the commercials to be over and for *Vince Vinelli's Worst Criminals Ever!* to come back on.

Everyone except for Grandma and Grandpa Tickler. They loved the commercials.

"Oh, it's the cow that wears purple glasses

commercial!" said Grandma Tickler from her E-Z chair recliner. "I love the cow with purple glasses!"

Grandma Tickler held a jar of jelly beans on her lap, eating them one by one. Whenever she found a black jelly bean, she gave it to Grandpa Tickler.

"Ayuh," said Grandpa from his own E-Z chair recliner.

"That's true, Irving," said Grandma. "The cow really does see better with purple glasses."

Most of the time, Grandpa Tickler only spoke one word: "ayuh." "Ayuh" meant "yes," but for Grandpa Tickler it could also mean a thousand other things. Luckily Grandma Tickler understood nine hundred and ninety-nine of them.

As for Charlie, he was trying to rehearse for tomorrow.

He had to do well tomorrow.

He didn't want to think about what would happen if he didn't do well tomorrow.

But it was hard to move his arms and practice his sign language with his parents sitting so quality-time close to him. Plus the criminals, their crimes, and the commercials were at full volume (even though the closed captions were on), making it hard for Charlie to concentrate.

"*Vince Vinelli*," Mrs. Tickler remarked during the cow commercial, "seems like a very violent show to be watching during our quality time with Charlie. Don't you agree, Alistair?"

"Indeed I do, Myra," said Mr. Tickler. He held up the current book he was reading: *How to be a Great Parent in Only Seven Days!*

"This book clearly states that violent shows are not good for children. Or adults," added Mr. Tickler. He wrote himself a note in his parenting notebook. He and Mrs. Tickler were learning how to be good parents to Charlie, and that meant lots of reading and note-taking.

Normally Charlie would have agreed with his parents—violent shows are not good for children.

But Charlie *had* to watch Vince Vinelli.

And there were lots of shows to watch, for in addition to the regular Friday night program, there were *Vince Vinelli Special Edition!* episodes as well.

When Vince Vinelli came back on, he leaned into the camera with a solemn look.

"Viewers, I want to take a short break from our worst criminals to ask you an important question." Vince looked off in the distance as if gathering his thoughts. Then he nodded and returned his gaze to the camera.

"Have you ever," asked Vince, "wanted to be a detective but didn't know how to start?"

"Yes!" said Grandma.

"Ayuh!" said Grandpa.

"Well, stop wanting right now," Vince told them.

"Because for only nine dollars and ninety-nine cents you can buy Vince Vinelli's When Crime Is a Fact, Good People Act detective kit. Inside this box is everything two people need to look like a pair of real detectives—for only nine ninety-nine!"

"Nine ninety-nine? That's a bargain!" said Grandma. She put down the jelly beans, reached for the pencil and newspaper on the table next to her, and wrote down the phone number flashing on the screen.

"But, Grandma," said Charlie, "it's nine ninety-nine *a month* for *twelve months*. See the tiny words under the flashing numbers?"

Charlie stopped practicing long enough to do the math in his head. *Turn the nine ninety-nine into a ten, and then multiply the ten by twelve. . . .*

"That's almost one hundred and twenty dollars," said Charlie.

"And if you order right now," continued Vince, "I'll throw in a Vince Vinelli's Good People Do Good Things certificate absolutely free!"

"Not absolutely free," said Charlie, "because you still have to pay nine ninety-nine a month for twelve months."

But Grandma Tickler wasn't listening. Grandma Tickler loved to buy things advertised on television.

"Yvette!" Grandma yelled for their housekeeper. "Where's my purse? Irving, we have to order that kit right now or we won't get the Good People certificate. And we're good people!"

"Stop shouting, Irma," said Yvette as she came into the living room. "It's right here."

"You can't buy that, Mother," said Mr. Tickler. "It's a waste of money!"

"But it's their money," said Yvette. "They can buy what they like—as silly as it might be."

"It's not silly!" said Grandma. "We need those detective outfits! How else are we going to fight crime?"

"You're not," said Yvette. "Just because someone looks like a detective that doesn't make them a detective."

But once again Grandma Tickler wasn't listening. She reached for the phone next to her E-Z chair recliner as another commercial came on.

Yvette sat down in the rocking chair next to the couch.

"Has he read any letters yet?" Yvette asked Charlie.

"After these commercials," said Charlie. "I hope."

When Vince Vinelli had announced that he would be reading fan letters at the end of each show, Charlie's best friend, Frog, immediately began writing him a letter every day. Frog not only told Vince how much she loved his show, she also told him all about herself. Frog told him her dream was to become a detective. Frog couldn't tell Vince that she already was a detective because she and Charlie had to keep the first case they solved a secret.

Charlie supposed that Vince Vinelli must get

thousands of letters, but he still watched every episode, hoping Vince would read one of the letters Frog had sent. He knew how much it would mean to her.

Charlie continued practicing his sign language. He could see what he needed to do in his head. He just hoped his head would tell his hands what to do when the time came.

What would happen if his head forgot?

After the commercials about a skateboarding cat and a medicine that would help your headache but possibly paralyze you, *Vince Vinelli's Worst Criminals Ever!* came back on.

"It's now time," said Vince, "for that special part of my show that viewers have come to love—Vince Vinelli Fan Letter Time!"

Charlie stopped practicing. "This is it!" said Charlie. "Fingers crossed!"

Charlie, Yvette, and Grandpa crossed their fingers. They always crossed their fingers at this part of the show. Even Grandma, who was waiting to place her order, crossed her fingers on one hand while holding the phone with the other.

"Why are we crossing our fingers?" asked Mrs. Tickler.

"For Frog," said Charlie.

"Who's Frog?" asked Mr. Tickler.

"His best friend," snapped Yvette.

Charlie's parents dutifully crossed their fingers, too.

"I love it when my fans write to me," said Vince. "Of course, I mostly love it when they write *about* me." Vince chuckled but quickly grew serious again. "Sometimes, though, my fans write about themselves. It's important that I read those letters too, especially when the letters are from kids—"

Charlie squeezed his crossed fingers tighter.

"—because kids have dreams, just like adults do!"

In his mind Charlie signed "*dream.*" Ever since he had started at Castle School for the Deaf, Charlie thought about sign language all the time.

"And kids with dreams," continued Vince, "have been writing me letters—"

Charlie held his breath.

"—such as this little girl who wrote me a letter—"

Charlie squeezed every single part of his body as hard as he could.

"—a little girl named—"

Say it, Charlie thought. Say Frog's name.

"—Francine Castle!"

"FROG!" Charlie, Yvette, and Grandma Tickler screamed at the same time.

"AYUH!" yelled Grandpa Tickler.

Charlie and Yvette jumped up and down. Grandma waved the phone receiver around. Grandpa pumped a fist in the air. Mr. and Mrs. Tickler, unsure of what was happening, politely clapped.

Vince Vinelli held up Frog's letter, written on her favorite frog stationery, in his very tan hands.

"Yes, viewers," said Vince, "little Francine Castle, also known as Frog, wrote me a letter. Little Froggy told me her dream is to become a detective!"

Why did Vince Vinelli keep calling Frog "little"? Charlie wondered. And why was he calling her Froggy? Nobody called her Froggy.

Vince looked deeply into the camera. "Little girl, little Froggy, keep your little dream alive—"

Charlie desperately wished Vince would stop saying the word "little."

"—because," said Vince, "maybe, just maybe, you will become a detective someday. But if you order Vince Vinelli's When Crime Is a Fact, Good People Act detective kit"—Vince flashed his blinding smile—"then you definitely will!"

The camera panned over to Vince Vinelli's When Crime Is a Fact, Good People Act detective kit, sitting next to Vince in its bright red box. He gave the box a little pat.

"Viewers," said Vince. "Little Froggy told me she is deaf and communicates in American Sign Language. So for little deaf Froggy I learned one sign—one special sign that describes her."

Please, Charlie silently begged, let the sign be *"powerful"* or *"amazing."*

Vince touched his index and middle fingers to his chin, thumb extended, and brushed his chin with his fingers twice. "*Cute!*" Vince Vinelli signed and then spoke.

"How nice!" said his mother.

"Very!" said his father.

"No," Charlie groaned.

"Because," said Vince, "that's what this fan letter is, and that's what you are, little Froggy—"

"Stop," said Charlie.

"—very, very—"

"Don't," said Charlie.

"—*cute!*" Vince Vinelli signed it once more.

"So sweet!" said Mrs. Tickler.

"And such an honor," said Mr. Tickler. "Vince Vinelli is very famous, you know."

Grandma covered the phone with her hand. "Frog isn't cute, is she, Irving?"

"Ayuh," said Grandpa.

"I didn't think so," said Grandma.

"You know what Frog is?" said Yvette. "Frog is furious right now, that's what Frog is."

Charlie agreed. But at least, he told himself, Frog couldn't hear Vince Vinelli's tone of voice. But just then the TV captions included this at the end:

(*Vince Vinelli is speaking in a voice that adults use to talk to very little children.*)

Charlie sighed. Frog was definitely furious.

2. Library

"We'll be gone just two weeks this time," Mrs. Tickler told Charlie the next morning as she closed her suitcase. "But don't worry—we'll keep up with our parental studies."

"We'll visit the library," said Mr. Tickler. "There are wonderful libraries in Texas!" He made the sign for "*library*" by forming the letter *L* and circling it sideways twice.

"And wonderful bookstores, too!" added his mother. "We ordered some parenting books from Blythe and Bone Bookshop, but they haven't arrived yet."

"I wish they had!" said his father, glancing at the

stack of library books on his nightstand. "Because Miss Tweedy said we're not to take any library books across state lines."

"I think," said Charlie, "you're allowed to take library books anywhere. You just have to return them on time."

"Well, better safe than sorry," said Mr. Tickler. He tucked his parenting notebook in his carry-on bag. "But I'll continue taking plenty of notes, Charlie. We'll get this parenting thing right yet!"

Charlie's parents loved to travel everywhere and help animals. They had helped piping plovers in Montana, northern hairy-nosed wombats in Australia, and giant golden moles in South Africa. Now, however, even as they were preparing to leave again, they wanted to learn about children so they could also help Charlie. They were certain the answer could be found in books.

• • •

Grandma and Grandpa Tickler were in the kitchen eating breakfast, with a deck of cards waiting on the table when Charlie and his parents came downstairs.

"Good-bye, Mother. Good-bye, Father," said Mr. Tickler. "We're off to Texas!"

"Texas blind salamanders need our help," said Mrs. Tickler. "Texas blind salamanders are too often ignored. We plan to give them plenty of time and attention!"

Yvette stopped washing dishes. She turned around to stare at Mrs. Tickler. Then she turned back to the sink, shaking her head.

"Well, take as long as you want," said Grandma as she ate her oatmeal. "We love having Charlie here with us."

"Ayuh," said Grandpa. He reached over and patted Charlie's hand.

"And we'll be busy solving mysteries as soon as our detective kit arrives!" added Grandma. "Now, Charlie, you'll have time for a game of cards before you leave for school, won't you?"

Charlie nodded. "What game?"

"Concentration," decided Grandma.

In the card game Concentration, you laid out all fifty-two cards facedown on the table. Then you turned them over two at a time, trying to find a match. You had to remember where the cards were—see them in your mind even though they were facedown. Concentration required a lot of concentration, which Charlie did not have this morning. But Grandma Tickler loved to win, so it wasn't a bad thing for him not to concentrate.

Charlie helped carry his parents' suitcases outside. Herman, the wizened little driver, got out of his taxi, took one look at the size of the Ticklers' suitcases, and promptly got back in.

Charlie loaded the suitcases into the trunk.

"I just realized something," said his father as he closed the trunk lid. "Today is Saturday. Why are you going to school on Saturday?"

"Maybe Charlie just loves learning, Alistair!" said his mother. "I know I do!"

"No," said Charlie. "I told you. Don't you remember?"

Charlie had, in fact, told his parents many times. The problem was they didn't write it down in their parenting notes, and it wasn't in their parenting books.

"Tonight is the Fall Extravaganza," Charlie reminded them. "I have to get to school early to practice and help set up."

"How fun!" said Mrs. Tickler. "But you don't look happy about it. In fact, you look worried. Doesn't Charlie look worried, Alistair?"

Mr. Tickler peered into Charlie's face. "Yes," he decided. "He certainly does."

"What do our parenting books say to do when your child looks worried?" asked Mrs. Tickler.

"I took notes," said Mr. Tickler. "But my notebook is inside my carry-on bag, which is inside the trunk of the taxi. Should I get it out?"

"Dad—" Charlie tried to speak.

"Yes, you should," said Mrs. Tickler. "This is a parenting moment, which means we need those parenting notes!"

"Mom, I'm—"

"Open the trunk!" Mr. Tickler called to Herman.

"Dad, I'm—"

"I think he's asleep, Alistair." Mrs. Tickler tapped on Herman's window. Herman's forehead popped off the steering wheel.

Charlie sighed. "You're going to miss your flight," he said.

Mr. Tickler looked at his watch. "You're right, Charlie. We'd better get going."

"But when we get back," said Mrs. Tickler, "we're going to spend lots of quality time with you— Alistair! The taxi!"

Herman, not realizing the Ticklers weren't in the taxi yet, had started slowly driving away. Charlie's parents jumped into the moving vehicle, stuck their heads out of the window, and waved.

"Good-bye, Charlie! Good-bye, darling! Don't worry! We'll call! We'll have quality phone conversations! Several of them!"

"Wear your seat belts!" Charlie yelled as Herman's taxi rolled down the street.

If Charlie's parents had taken the time to pay attention to him, he would have told them that he *was* worried.

He was worried about Frog because of what Vince Vinelli had said last night.

But most of all Charlie was worried about the Boney Hand.

3. The Boney Hand

Within the walls of Castle School for the Deaf, stories flourished and flowed. These stories were always swirling around Charlie. He could see them with his eyes, but he didn't understand most of them because they were shared in American Sign Language.

But two stories Charlie did know well.

The story behind the statue of Alice and Francine in the middle of the great hall.

And the story of the Boney Hand.

Charlie knew the story of Alice and Francine was true. It was the story of how the Castle family founded the Deaf school two hundred years ago. Frog's great-great-great (Charlie wasn't sure how many greats, but there were a lot) grandmother, Francine Castle, had been born Deaf. When her parents learned about the first Deaf school in America, they went to visit. There they met a girl named Alice, who taught Francine her first sign—*"frog."*

But the story of the Boney Hand? Charlie had no idea if it was really true. Here's what Charlie did know:

One hundred and fifty years ago, pirates sailed the Hudson River.

When children spotted a pirate flag, they ran inside their homes and warned their parents to hide their animals.

Because pirates stole puppies as they plundered.

Pirates snatched cows as they pillaged.

Nefarious, as Chief Paley would say.

Which means bad.

Pirates were bad people. Everyone could *see* the pirates were bad.

And the most feared pirate of all was Jeremiah Bone, also known as Boney Jack.

Boney Jack *looked* bad—very, very bad.

Which meant he was supposed to *be* bad.

Except he wasn't.

When the pirates pilfered a puppy, Boney Jack made sure the hound found its way back to its child.

When the pirates finished drinking their stolen milk, Boney Jack untied the cow and sent the bovine home.

Boney Jack never stole. He only returned.

This, of course, outraged the bad pirates. A good pirate was not allowed. All pirates must be bad.

So they plotted to get rid of him.

They bribed a wealthy, powerful landowner to falsely accuse Boney Jack of thievery. No one came to his defense. Everyone believed what was *said* about Boney Jack, instead of looking at *who* Boney Jack was and *what* he really did.

A pirate trial ensued.

Boney Jack was found guilty.

On a chilly fall day, Boney Jack was forced to walk the plank.

He sank to the bottom of the cold Hudson River.

The fish ate every morsel off Boney Jack's bones until only his skeleton remained.

But Boney Jack's story didn't end there.

When the moon was full, one of Boney Jack's bony hands left his bony skeleton. It crawled along the muddy bottom of the river. When it came to a bluff, its bony fingers clung to the rock and climbed upward to Castle School for the Deaf.

The hand inched its way to the graveyard.

And dragged itself into the church.

It was there the school caretaker found the bony hand crouched on the floor, covered in seaweed and mud. The caretaker walked slowly toward it.

He got closer.

And closer.

Until he was poised directly over the bony hand.

The caretaker bent down and picked it up.

Suddenly, the hand reared up on its bony bottom. It fingerspelled a message to the stunned caretaker, who keeled over in shock.

A teacher found him lying on the stone floor, next to the now motionless bony hand. As she gathered the caretaker in her arms, he used his last breath to tell her what the hand had said.

"It fingerspelled," the caretaker signed to the teacher, *"NO . . . ONE . . . SAW . . ."*

The caretaker's hands fell to his sides.

"No one saw WHAT?" the teacher asked.

But the caretaker died before he could finish the message.

What had the bony hand been trying to say?

No one saw . . . what?

To this day, it remains a mystery.

To this day, nobody—

"Charlie, watch out!"

Charlie had been walking in the village, thinking about the Legend of the Boney Hand, when he bumped into Elspeth Tweedy. Miss Tweedy held a large pot out at arm's length as something orange dribbled down the side.

"My goodness!" said Miss Tweedy. "I almost spilled Enid's pumpkin soup! And my sister makes the best pumpkin soup." Through her pointy eyeglasses, she gave Charlie a disapproving look.

"Sorry, Miss Tweedy," said Charlie.

Matilda Blythe was coming down the steps of the Pig and Soap Bed-and-Breakfast holding a box. "Hi, Charlie! If you're heading to the school, would you mind helping us carry these to the bookshop on your way?"

Matilda, along with her grandfather, Thelonious Bone, owned Blythe and Bone Bookshop.

"Sure," said Charlie. He took the box from Matilda, who went back up the steps of the Tweedys' bed-and-breakfast.

Elspeth and Enid Tweedy owned the Pig and Soap Bed-and-Breakfast. Elspeth Tweedy was also acting librarian of the Castle-on-the-Hudson Library and curator of the Castle-on-the-Hudson Museum, which Charlie had yet to see. Enid Tweedy owned the Naked Ewe, a knitting shop.

Enid came out of the Pig and Soap with a second soup pot. Knitting needles protruded from her apron pocket. Enid had used a knitting needle to protect Aggie Penderwick against Dex and Ray over the summer.

Enid had once told Charlie she always liked to have knitting needles with her—for safety when needed, and for knitting when not.

"Thanks, Enid." Matilda took the soup pot from her. "Maybe this will help Bone snap out of his mood."

"Sprinkle toasted pumpkin seeds on top," said Enid. "Toasted pumpkin seeds are essential." She waved to Charlie, patted her knitting needles inside her pocket, and went back inside.

It was a glorious autumn day—the sky bright blue, the air crisp and cool, and smelling of freshly brewed coffee. The village of Castle-on-the-Hudson was famous for having the most coffee shops per square block. Right now, it was also decorated with pumpkins and hay bales, cornstalks and scarecrows. Fall was Charlie's favorite time of year.

"I commend your mother and father, Charlie," said Miss Tweedy as they walked to the bookshop. "They seem determined to become experts in parenting. I told them anything they want to learn about being a good parent can be found in a book."

"I don't think that's how it works," said Matilda.

"What's in the box?" asked Charlie before Miss Tweedy could argue about Charlie's parents.

"Pig soap," Miss Tweedy answered. "My latest batch."

"What's pig soap?" Charlie asked. "Soap for pigs?"

Matilda giggled. Miss Tweedy sniffed.

"They are soaps in the shape of a pig," said Miss Tweedy. "They are for humans."

"We sell them at the bookshop," Matilda told Charlie.

"Books and pig soap go so well together," said Miss Tweedy.

"They do?" said Charlie.

"Certainly they do," she said. "People read in the bathtub. People wash with pig soap in the bathtub. There you are!"

"Makes sense to me," said Matilda. "Charlie, how's school going?"

This was Charlie's first year at Castle School for the Deaf, even though he was "hearing." It was Mrs. Castle, Frog's mother, who had insisted he attend school there because, she decided, Charlie needed them. And she was right.

So how was school going?

Charlie could say he loved school, which was one hundred million percent true. He could say it was different than any other school that he had ever attended, and Charlie had attended lots of schools.

Castle School for the Deaf wasn't different just because it was a Deaf school and used ASL. It was *special* different in so many other ways. But right now, Charlie was worried about letting everyone down—especially Frog and Mrs. Castle. So right now, school wasn't going that well.

"Fine," said Charlie.

"You know," Matilda told him, "I always wanted to go to school there, but I was hearing and I wasn't a Castle."

Until Charlie enrolled, the only hearing kids who had ever attended Castle School for the Deaf were Castle family members, like Oliver and Millie, Frog's hearing brother and sister.

Matilda nudged Charlie with her elbow. "You must be an honorary member of the Castle family."

Matilda had just said the best thing ever. Charlie took a moment to imagine the Castles as his real family. Then he immediately felt guilty about not wanting the family he did have.

They passed Junk and Stuff, Frog's favorite place to buy her "statement pieces," what Frog called the jewelry she wore every day. Nathan's Ice Cream Emporium wasn't open yet. Charlie wondered what vegetable-flavored ice cream Nate was concocting for the fall. Squash ice cream? Corn ice cream? Or maybe pumpkin ice cream, which sounded much better than the butterscotch broccoli ice cream he had tasted over the summer.

"Charlie," said Miss Tweedy, "you seemed lost in

thought when you bumped into me earlier. What were you thinking about?"

Miss Tweedy's question reminded Charlie to start worrying again.

"I was thinking," said Charlie, "about this." He curled his fingers into a claw shape, the sign for "*the Boney Hand.*"

Miss Tweedy stopped walking. The pumpkin soup sloshed inside the pot and once more dribbled down the side.

"Don't sign that," said Miss Tweedy. "Just seeing that unnerves me. It's a *horrendous* story because it involves"— her voice dropped to a whisper—"the *D* word."

"Death," said Matilda helpfully, in case Charlie didn't understand.

"Language, Matilda!" Miss Tweedy scolded.

"It is a scary story," agreed Charlie as they started walking again. Then he blurted out, "And it's even scarier because I'm one of the kids signing the story this year."

This was what had been worrying Charlie.

Every year, at the Fall Extravaganza, students signed two performances of the Legend of the Boney Hand while Mr. Willoughby, who was hearing, read it out loud. Mrs. Castle, who was Deaf, had been tutoring Charlie in ASL. She insisted Charlie was ready to sign a few lines in the performance.

It was one thing to sign with Frog or Mrs. Castle or another student. It was something else entirely to be signing in front of everyone. Charlie knew from past experience that it was always safer when you stuck to the edges. It was like playing the game of dodgeball, which was very popular at Charlie's last school. Some kids stood right in the middle, daring others to try to hit them with the ball. Other kids, like Charlie, tried to avoid being seen by staying away from the front and center. A hearing kid trying to sign in front of a Deaf school was a sure way to get a ball in the face.

"I love the Legend of the Boney Hand," said Matilda. "I wish I could go this year and watch you, but I have to be at the bookshop since Bone wants the night off. You're braver than I was at your age, Charlie," she said as they crossed the street. "I would never go near the Boney Hand when I went to the Fall Extravaganza."

"What do you mean?" said Charlie. "It's just a story. There is no Boney Hand."

"Oh, yes there is," said Miss Tweedy. "Edward Willoughby keeps that awful thing locked away all year. He takes the Boney Hand out only for the Fall Extravaganza."

"Whoa," said Charlie. "Wait a minute." Now he was the one to stop walking. "The Boney Hand is *real*?"

"Oh, it's real," said Matilda. "And it's spelled *B-O-N-E-Y* because the Boney Hand is supposedly the hand of our ancestor Jeremiah Bone. My grandfather despises the Fall Extravaganza for that reason. Bone refuses to attend the Legend of the Boney Hand performance because the hand is on display. He says it's disrespectful. But other family members, like my cousin Edward Willoughby, disagree."

"He's your cousin?" said Charlie. Mr. Willoughby was on the Board of Trustees at Castle School for the Deaf. He gave a lot of money to the school, and once a year directed and starred in the Legend of the Boney Hand. He was as cantankerous (Chief Paley's word) as Matilda was kind.

"Edward is part of the Bone family on his mother's side," said Matilda. "I'm surprised no one told you about all this."

"They probably did," said Charlie. He sighed as they began walking again.

The problem was Charlie was still new at sign language. And he didn't always have someone nearby to help him navigate the conversations around him, such as one of the school interpreters or Frog's brother, Oliver. When people signed directly to Charlie, they always slowed down because they knew he was just learning ASL. But when they signed to each other, they signed at their normal speed, and Charlie wasn't fluent enough to understand everything at that speed yet. So when everyone was talking about the Boney Hand, Charlie had completely missed the part about the hand being *real*. That was the price he paid for being signing-impaired in a Deaf world. He missed out on a lot of stuff.

"So if Jeremiah Bone is your real ancestor," Charlie said to Matilda, "does that mean the story of the Boney Hand is true? That the Boney Hand crawled out of the river and up the cliff to the graveyard and then finger-spelled the words 'No one saw . . .' to the caretaker, who died of shock?"

"Language, Charlie!" said Miss Tweedy. "And yes, it's absolutely true!"

"It's a *story*," said Matilda. "Stories describe how something felt, not how something exactly happened. This story has been told in our family and at the school for generations. It's taken on a meaning and a life of its own. So did it really happen? Who knows?"

"*I* know," said Miss Tweedy as they arrived at Blythe and Bone Bookshop. "It did happen. And that's exactly why I never attend the Fall Extravaganza. Because the Boney Hand is still alive! It can scuttle and scurry— here, there, and everywhere!"

"Elspeth, please," said Matilda as she balanced the soup pot on one knee, took out her keys, and opened the door.

"I would be afraid," Miss Tweedy called to Charlie as he followed Matilda into the bookshop. "Very afraid."

Matilda put the soup on the counter and took the

box of pig soap from Charlie. Then she placed her hands on his shoulders. Tattooed on Matilda's arm was a little girl holding a book. She had the same cloud of black curly hair as Matilda had.

"Charlie," said Matilda, "it's just a story, so stop worrying! That's an order!"

Then, as if Matilda could see what was really bothering him, she added, "It's not easy learning a new language. And you're in a new school as well, so there's that." Matilda took her hands off Charlie's shoulders and pointed to him. "There are no accidents. You're at that school for a reason. And Frog will be there for you tonight."

Ever since Charlie had started at Castle School for the Deaf, Frog had been his anchor. When Charlie was with Frog, Charlie belonged because Frog belonged. She was always helping him with sign language and included Charlie wherever they went. She calmed him down during the Legend of the Boney Hand rehearsals, signing Charlie's part along with him so he could follow her.

Matilda was right.

Of course Frog would be there for him.

She was always there for him.

"Remember," said Matilda, pointing to the words on her tattoo, "you are not alone."

4. Yes

Like Charlie, there were other students in the village who rode the gondola to school instead of living in the dorms. Several of them were in line at the gondola station when he arrived. As Charlie watched their hands, arms, shoulders, and faces easily conversing in ASL, he wished with all his heart he understood everything they were saying.

Mr. Simple locked the gondola door behind the last rider. He flashed his giant round signal lamp toward the castle, letting them know the gondola was preparing to leave. Modern technology such as cell phones simply did not work in the village of Castle-on-the-Hudson—only up at the castle. No one knew why, and no one, Charlie noticed, seemed to care very much—except for Augusta V. Paley, chief of police.

As the gondola lurched into the air, Charlie took a deep breath and tried not to think about the Boney Hand, which was hard to do with the two visitors sitting across from him.

"I love coming to the castle every fall to hear the Legend of the Boney Hand, don't you?" one woman said to the other.

"Do you think it's true?" the other woman asked. "About the Boney Hand being alive?"

"Of course it's true! Just like the Headless Horseman is true! Why wouldn't it be true?"

Charlie knew about the Headless Horseman thanks to Ruthella Jones, one of Frog's best friends. Ruthella had read "The Legend of Sleepy Hollow," and then retold the scary story to Charlie.

A finger tapped Charlie on the knee.

"Can you hear me?" the woman asked loudly, exaggerating her lip movements.

Charlie nodded. He almost laughed at how silly she looked.

"Don't you think the legend is true?" the woman asked. "About the Boney Hand?"

Both women looked at him expectantly, waiting for his answer.

"No," said Charlie firmly. "I think it's just a story."

The woman snorted. She whispered to her friend, "What does he know? He's not Deaf like them." The woman tilted her head toward the students signing to one another. "He doesn't even go to that school!" she added.

I *do* go to that school! Charlie wanted to yell. It's my school, too!

But he looked out the windows instead.

From high above the Hudson River, the view was spectacular. The village was nestled in a valley of orange, yellow, and red trees. The river sparkled in the sunlight. Two people paddled kayaks in the water as a sailboat glided by them. Charlie turned his head toward the castle sitting on a bluff, grand and glorious.

Charlie had parents who wanted to be with animals more than they wanted to be with him.

He had grandparents who loved watching television, visiting doctors, and now (thanks to Charlie) playing card games.

But he also had Castle School for the Deaf.

Charlie belonged to that school, even if he was hearing. He wouldn't let his school down tonight.

As for Frog, maybe she wasn't too upset about what Vince Vinelli had said.

Maybe, just maybe (Charlie crossed his fingers),

Frog had missed watching *Vince Vinelli's Worst Criminals Ever!* last night.

• • •

Wendell Finch was one of the students helping at the gondola today. Wendell was shorter than Charlie, with thick, round glasses that gave him the look of a wise and eager owl.

"*Hi, Charlie!*" signed Wendell as Charlie stepped off the gondola. "*It's here! The best day of the year is finally here!*"

The Fall Extravaganza was the best day of the year because it was the day Boney Jack's story was retold. Wendell wanted everyone to remember that Boney Jack had once done secret good deeds for people in the Hudson Valley. And every fall, in the spirit of Boney Jack, Wendell also did secret good deeds. It was the worst-kept secret because everyone knew it was Wendell, but everyone pretended they had no idea.

"*Happy Boney Hand Day!*" signed Charlie. He had been practicing this just so he could sign it to Wendell today.

Wendell beamed. "*Happy Boney Hand Day to you, too!*"

"*I just learned,*" signed Charlie, "*that the Boney Hand is a real hand!*"

"*I know!*" Wendell signed slowly and clearly for Charlie. "*Isn't it wonderful? We have Boney Jack's hand to help us remember him!*"

Charlie watched as Wendell flashed the signal light several times toward the village across the river, sending a message to Mr. Simple. When the gondola was loaded again with people, Wendell would send another message.

The castle grounds were a flurry of students, teachers, and staff, preparing for the Fall Extravaganza—carving pumpkins, making scarecrows, putting out bales of hay, and setting up fires for s'mores and the telling of ghost stories. Obie, the DeafBlind castle caretaker, stood in the middle of all of this busyness with his wild white hair and his new dog, Max, at his side, calmly directing everyone.

Students checked in with Obie by putting their smaller hands under his larger ones to ask him what they should do next. Obie's coworker, Darius, stood next to Obie with one hand on his back, letting Obie know what was happening around him, quickly telling him the things he did not see with his eyes. After lunch, Charlie would help Obie in the barn.

Frog's six-year-old sister Millie and her huge dog, Bear, a Newfoundland, ran up to Charlie. Millie flung her arms around his waist as Bear slurped Charlie's hand with his tongue. Millie finally let go of her hug, and Bear flopped down on the grass, having used up all his saliva on Charlie.

"I don't like Vince Vinelli!" Millie told Charlie. "Frog is not cute! I'm cute!"

Charlie knew Millie was not allowed to watch Vince Vinelli. That meant Frog had watched it.

"I was hoping Frog hadn't seen the show," said Charlie as Frog's older brother, Oliver, came over.

"Of course Frog saw it," said Oliver. "She never misses an episode." He put an arm around Charlie. "Your mission this morning is to cheer up Frog enough to come to rehearsal."

"Wait—Frog might not come to rehearsal?" said Charlie.

"She didn't take last night very well," said Oliver. "And you know how Frog is—when she's mad about something, she can't think of anything else."

Charlie's worst fear was happening. Even just *thinking* about being without Frog at rehearsal left him feeling unanchored, floating on a life raft in the ocean with no land in sight.

"If she's not there, Mr. Willoughby will have a fit," continued Oliver. "And if Mr. Willoughby has a fit, Mom will have a fit. You know she gets intense this time of year," Oliver added as they walked toward the castle.

"Just like she got before the Founders' Day Dinner," said Charlie as he envisioned himself at tonight's performance, forgetting his lines and staring blankly into the audience.

"Exactly," said Oliver. "But let's not kid ourselves—basically, the whole year is full of days with Mom getting intense. But especially today. With Mom, you have to know her 'especially' days."

Charlie knew visitors came from all over to tour the castle, and to see and hear the Legend of the Boney Hand. That was why the whole school had been cleaning and decorating the castle for a week, as well as practicing the Legend of the Boney Hand. Many of the visitors would be hearing people who didn't know sign language. Outsiders, Mrs. Castle called them.

Bear was walking between Charlie and Millie. Charlie rested a hand on Bear's glossy black fur.

"Did you know the Boney Hand is real, Charlie?" Millie shivered. "It's scary!"

"I just found out it was real," said Charlie. "I missed that somehow."

"You're doing really well with signing, Charlie," said Millie as she patted his arm.

"But not well enough," said Oliver as they entered the castle. "And that's why you have Boris."

"Who's Boris?" asked Charlie.

Oliver pointed to a big guy standing near the Flying Hands Café, staring at his cell phone. "Boris is your interpreter this week," said Oliver.

"I don't need an interpreter!" said Charlie.

"Oh, but you do," said Oliver.

Bear trotted over to Boris, nudging him with his nose. Boris put his phone away and rubbed Bear's head with both hands.

"I forgot!" said Millie. "I promised Obie that Bear would play with Max today!" Millie turned to leave, but Bear didn't follow her because Boris was now kneeling and massaging Bear's neck and back. Charlie could have sworn Bear was smiling.

"Bear!" yelled Millie. "Come!"

Bear woke from his blissful state and reluctantly pushed up to his paws. He looked up at Boris, waiting.

"Bear!" Millie yelled again.

Bear waited.

"Go with Millie," Boris told him.

Finally, Bear turned and lumbered over to Millie.

"Bear listens to me," she told Boris. "Not you!"

"Sorry." Boris shrugged. "Dogs love me."

"Bear loves *me*," said Millie as she walked away. Bear glanced once more at Boris and then followed.

Charlie turned to Oliver. "I don't need an interpreter," said Charlie again. "And if I do, I have Miss Davenport." Miss Davenport sometimes interpreted Charlie's classes. "Or I have you, Oliver," added Charlie. "No offense, Boris."

"None taken," said Boris. "I'm heading to film school

in a few months. This castle looks like a movie set." Boris held up his phone and began panning around the great hall.

"Look, Charlie," said Oliver, "my debt to Frog is paid off. Besides, interpreting is hard work and it doesn't make me happy. Baking makes me happy. And there are still a zillion pumpkin and apple pies to be baked for tonight. And you miss a lot," Oliver told him, not unkindly. "Having Boris around will help you understand more. Besides," he added as Mrs. Castle approached, "it's what Mom wants."

Mrs. Castle had another long to-do list with her, just as she had for the Founders' Day Dinner. When she saw Charlie, she hurried over to hug him. Mrs. Castle always made a humming noise in her throat when she hugged people. Deaf hugs were strong and solid. And Mrs. Castle's hugs were the best hugs of all.

Mrs. Castle asked Boris to interpret for her.

"See?" Mrs. Castle signed to Charlie as Boris spoke what she said. *"Now you don't need pen and paper if you don't understand something—you have Boris. Boris will be our interpreting intern for this week. Boris's mother is Deaf and a dear friend of mine. She hopes her son will consider interpreting as a professional career. Perhaps he will go to college to become an interpreter instead of this crazy idea of going to film school."*

Boris interpreted what Mrs. Castle said. He didn't even make a face at Mrs. Castle's comment about him. Oliver would never have done that. He would have made a face, rolled his eyes, and then added his own opinion. Everything interpreters are not supposed to do.

"I don't need another interpreter!" signed Charlie to Mrs. Castle. Charlie especially did not want someone like Boris, who was quite large, following him around. It would be like having a babysitter. Or a bodyguard. Boris would make him stand out. Charlie did not want to stand out, especially not any more than he already did.

Oliver shook his head behind his mother's back. He was reminding Charlie about his mother's intensity and that today was an "especially day."

"Yes," Mrs. Castle signed to Charlie, *"you do."* Mrs. Castle signed *"yes"* by making a fist and nodding the fist up and down. Charlie saw she had some red paint on the back of her hand.

"Now," she continued, *"please go talk to Frog. She's taking this Vince Vinelli thing much too seriously. It was an honor he read her letter on the show! She should be thrilled, not 'in the depths of despair,' as she says."*

Boris spoke everything Mrs. Castle signed.

It was true. It was much easier to have Boris's voice in his ear than to work so hard to understand ASL. And it was much faster than writing. Most importantly,

Mrs. Castle wanted him to work with Boris. Charlie couldn't say no to Mrs. Castle.

"Okay," signed Charlie.

"Good!" signed Mrs. Castle. *"Remember, having an interpreter will support your learning of ASL—"*

She stopped signing and stared at someone. It was a man entering the Flying Hands Café. He wore paint-splattered clothes. Mrs. Castle didn't seem intense anymore—now she seemed anxious, a feeling Charlie knew too well.

Finally, Mrs. Castle looked back at Charlie and gave him her *"I'm-here-if-you-need-me"* sign before hurrying into the Flying Hands Café.

The sign *"I'm-here-if-you-need-me"* was really the *"I love you"* sign, but as Oliver had explained to Charlie, it could mean so much more. And one way Mrs. Castle used the sign was to let Charlie know she was here if he needed her.

"Time to go cheer up Frog," said Oliver. "Rehearsal starts in thirty minutes."

Charlie took a deep breath. *"Okay,"* he signed and turned to leave.

"Where are you going?" asked Oliver.

"Up to Frog's room," said Charlie.

"When Frog is in the depths of despair, she doesn't go to her room," said Oliver. "Frog goes to the graveyard."

5. Sorry

The headstones tilted at odd angles. The wind rattled the leaves. Even though it was a sunny day, it didn't feel sunny inside the graveyard.

"This," said Boris, "would be the perfect place to film a horror movie."

"I know," said Charlie. And it would feel as if Charlie were *in* a horror movie if he couldn't get Frog to leave the cemetery.

"Frog helped me set up my time-lapse camera to shoot the full moon rising last night," said Boris. "Then she went to watch that show with the guy with the big teeth and fake tan. Bummer what he said."

Through the trees, Charlie could see students string-ing lights from the branches in front of the stone church. "You don't have to come with me," said Charlie. "I can talk to Frog myself."

"But I'm supposed to interpret," said Boris. "You heard Mrs. Castle. You don't want to make her mad."

"Consider this your break time," said Charlie.

Boris shrugged. "Okay. But text me if you need me. You have a phone, right?"

Charlie did have a phone, but he rarely used it. Cell phones didn't work in the village, only at the castle. At school Charlie often forgot he had a phone, espe-cially since Frog didn't have one. She lost her phone last summer, and her parents refused to buy her a new one. Frog said she would rather save her money for jewelry and books.

Charlie showed Boris his phone.

"Wow, this is old." Boris examined it as if he'd just found an artifact from long ago. "Tiny, too."

Boris took Charlie's phone and sent himself a text message. He handed it back to Charlie, pulled out his own large and new-looking phone, and leaned against the headstone of Beatrice R. Bellows, beloved wife of Horace T. Bellows. The words on her headstone read:

I AM WATCHING YOU.

Charlie hoped she wasn't. Beatrice, he was sure,

would not consider it respectful to use her headstone as a backrest.

Charlie continued on the path that wound through the graveyard. Leaves twirled off trees, twisting and spinning to the ground. A crow cawed from the end of a branch. Frog was probably writing an angry letter to Vince Vinelli right now, telling him what she thought. She just needed to get that letter written before she came to rehearsal, Charlie thought.

But Frog was not writing a letter. She was sitting by the headstone of her favorite author, D. J. McKinnon, her head bent over a book. A leaf landed on the page she was reading. As she brushed it away, she glanced up and spotted Charlie.

Frog was crying.

Charlie was so shocked, he stopped walking.

Charlie had thought Frog would be furious, enraged, angry, or fighting mad at what Vince Vinelli had said.

He had not expected this.

Frog quickly brushed the tears away with the back of her hand. She slammed the book shut and jumped to her feet. Grabbing a rake lying on the ground, she began scraping at leaves.

That's when Charlie was shocked a second time.

Frog wasn't wearing any jewelry. No diamond brooch glinted in the sunlight. No ruby earrings dangled from her ears. No pearl necklace swung around as Frog jerked the rake. Frog without her statement piece was harder for Charlie to see than Frog with tears.

Frog's eyes stayed on the leaf pile she was building.

Charlie tried to get her attention. He put his hand down low and waved it around. Frog would see his hand from the corner of her eye, wouldn't she? Charlie came as close as he dared to Frog, tapped her on her shoulder, and quickly jumped back. It was a good thing he did because Frog whipped around with the rake.

The two friends glared and stared. Frog did the glaring. Charlie did the staring. Charlie had never dealt with Frog being sad before. He wasn't sure what to do or what to say. Then he signed the only thing he could think of, the only thing he needed Frog to know.

"I'm sorry," signed Charlie, circling his fist flat on his chest. *"I'm really, really sorry."*

Frog tossed the rake on the ground and hung her head. She pressed the heels of her hands to her eyes and then looked up at Charlie.

"How could Vince Vinelli have said that?" signed Frog. She signed some other stuff, but Charlie didn't catch what she said. He pulled out his notebook and pen and handed them to Frog. He felt bad doing it. To Frog's credit, she only gave a small sigh about having to slow down her communication with writing.

How, wrote Frog, *could Vince Vinelli not see who I*

am? I wrote him dozens of letters. But all he saw was that I was cute.

Frog handed the notebook and pen back to Charlie and began raking again.

"He doesn't even know you," signed Charlie. *"So how can he see you?"*

Frog threw the rake down.

"He would know me," signed Frog, *"if he paid attention."*

"So write him another letter," Charlie told her. *"An even better letter!"*

Frog shook her head and reached for the rake, but Charlie wiggled his fingers.

"Wait!" he signed.

Frog waited. And while she waited, she looked so sad.

Charlie hated seeing her like this. What could he say to Frog that would make a difference? How could he make her feel better? Charlie glanced down at the book Frog had been reading: *Dorrie McCann and the Invisible Girl* by D. J. McKinnon. Frog loved Dorrie McCann, who was also Deaf.

That was it.

Some people, wrote Charlie, *didn't see Dorrie McCann as a detective, either.*

Charlie had no idea if this was true. He had only, after all, read one Dorrie McCann book. Frog considered this. Finally, she started to sign *"True."* Then she dropped her hand and shrugged.

"*So what if that's true?*" signed Frog. "*I'm not Dorrie McCann.*"

Frog fingerspelled DORRIE MCCANN slowly so Charlie would understand. Then she began raking again.

Charlie looked at his watch. Mr. Willoughby did not tolerate tardiness. And this was the final rehearsal before the performance. But Frog also had to be there. She had the most lines. And she needed to be there for Charlie. There was no way he could do this without her. Charlie tapped Frog on the shoulder.

"*What?*" signed Frog with one hand without looking at him.

How was Charlie supposed to tell Frog "what" if Frog didn't look? He tapped her on the shoulder again. When Frog glanced over, Charlie pointed toward the church.

Frog shook her head.

"*Not me,*" she signed. "*I'm staying here.*"

She threw down the rake once more, picked up her book, and sat down by D. J. McKinnon's headstone. She scooted back until she leaned against the headstone, just like Boris had. Frog crossed her legs, opened the book, and began reading.

But Charlie knew she really wasn't. He waved his hand in front of her face.

"*How long are you going to stay?*" signed Charlie. Maybe Frog just needed a few minutes by herself. Then she would be ready.

Frog studied the graveyard as she thought about Charlie's question.

"Forever," she signed. Then she turned another page and continued to pretend-read.

But what about me? Charlie wanted to ask her.

What if I fail? What if I forget my part?

Mr. Willoughby would blame him for ruining the Legend of the Boney Hand.

The other students would blame him.

Charlie would never fit in.

And Mrs. Castle would be disappointed. That hurt Charlie most of all.

Charlie started to sign something else, but Frog had a Frog look on her face—the look that said, "I've made up my mind and no one is going to change it." Charlie had seen that look many times before. While Frog turned another page in her book, Charlie turned and walked back to Boris.

Boris dragged his eyes away from his phone. "You okay?" he asked Charlie.

No, Charlie wasn't okay.

His anchor was gone. He was floating away, adrift on a wide-open sea—

Someone nudged his shoulder.

It was Frog.

She stomped ahead, leading the way to rehearsal.

"Yeah," Charlie told Boris. "I'm okay."

6. Bully

Frog glowered at anyone who dared to look at her before sitting down in a pew between Charlie and Ruthella Jones.

The students turned to one another and began to whisper-sign, keeping their hands low and close to their bodies, turning their backs so Frog couldn't see what they were saying.

Everyone was discussing what Vince Vinelli had said about Frog last night.

Boris sat down behind Charlie. Ruthella opened a book and began reading. Ruthella read books at breakfast, lunch, dinner, and every moment in between. Ruthella knew about everything. At least everything you could learn from reading books. As Frog slumped in the pew, Charlie studied his script.

He only had two lines.

The first line was the Boney Hand's message to the caretaker: NO ONE SAW. Charlie was to fingerspell this just like the Boney Hand had fingerspelled it.

Then Charlie was supposed to sign, *"Saw what? Nobody knows!"*

When no one was watching him, Charlie did fine. When all eyes were on him, Charlie's hands and brain felt like they were moving through molasses.

Charlie glanced at Frog. She was here, but she wasn't really *here*. He hoped Frog would return by the time Mr. Willoughby arrived and rehearsal started.

Charlie then realized how selfish that was, thinking only of himself. Being a detective meant everything to Frog. To have someone like Vince Vinelli make her dream seem childlike and silly hurt her. A lot.

The church door slammed. Charlie jumped. When he looked over his shoulder, he saw Rupert Miggs grinning at him.

If Charlie could pick just one thing to change about Castle School for the Deaf, Rupert Miggs would be it.

Frog had taught Charlie the sign for *"bully."* You

make the letter *Y* with one hand and the number 1 with the other. You bump the knuckles of the *Y* upward against the middle of the number 1 twice. *Bully.*

Rupert Miggs was the worst kind of bully—a stealth bully. Stealth bullies were bullies who didn't *seem* like bullies. They didn't look like bullies. Rupert, in fact, looked like a perfectly nice boy. Lots of people liked stealth bullies, especially grown-ups. But in reality they were mean kids who did mean things in a hidden and underhanded way.

When Charlie first met Rupert, Rupert had been nice to him. Then slowly the stealth bully inside Rupert came out. The fact that Charlie was hearing gave Rupert lots of opportunities to be mean.

Rupert slamming the church door hard was one example.

Some hard-of-hearing kids had heard it, too.

Some of the other kids felt it.

But only Charlie, who was hearing, had jumped.

After grinning at Charlie, Rupert turned to Jasper Dill, the boy who had come in with him. Jasper was Rupert's best friend, but today it was Jasper's turn to be bullied, even though Jasper was a lot taller, bigger, and stronger than Rupert.

"*You smell,*" Rupert signed to Jasper.

"*That's not true!*" signed Jasper. "*I showered last night!*"

"*Did you use soap?*" Rupert asked.

"*Yes!*" signed Jasper.

"*I don't think so.*" Rupert waved the palm of his hand past his nose as he sat down. Several kids laughed. Rupert laughed, too. He had a friendly laugh if you didn't know he was a stealth bully. Charlie hated that laugh.

Boris was looking at his phone and missed this conversation. But Charlie didn't need an interpreter for bullies. Charlie understood bullies perfectly.

He also felt bad for Jasper, but not that bad because Jasper could be mean, too. Rupert stopped teasing him, reached over, and flicked Wendell Finch on the back of his head. Rupert did it so fast you almost didn't see it.

Wendell Finch never bothered anyone.

Wendell's eyes widened. He turned around and stared with fear at Rupert. He looked ready to cry.

Normally it would have been Frog to tell Rupert to stop. Charlie was certain if Frog ever played dodgeball, she would be the kid in the front line daring the other team to hit her. But Frog was slouching with her arms crossed, staring at the floor.

It was one thing for Charlie to ignore Rupert when Rupert was bullying *him*; it was something else entirely to ignore Rupert when he was bullying someone smaller and weaker than Charlie.

Rupert flicked the back of Wendell's head again.

Charlie was gathering his bravery to stand and sign "*Stop!*" when Mr. Willoughby entered the church.

Rupert stopped flicking. Charlie sighed with relief. Ruthella hid her book beneath her script, and Boris put away his phone.

Mr. Willoughby wore a black pirate hat with a feather, a white ruffled shirt, and a stuffed parrot on one shoulder. He walked down the aisle like a bride at her wedding. He waited to sign until each student was looking at him. Frog was the last one to look up after Charlie nudged her three times.

"This," signed Mr. Willoughby as Boris interpreted, *"is our final rehearsal before our performance tonight. A performance that honors not only our school, but my family."*

Mr. Willoughby's signing was grand and dramatic, like a king addressing his subjects.

"I expect perfection—absolute perfection—tonight," signed Mr. Willoughby. *"Make sure you wear your school shirts and"* —he looked down his nose— *"make sure they are clean."*

Mr. Willoughby pointed an accusing finger at the students he didn't trust to have a clean shirt. One of those students was Jasper. Rupert snickered.

"This evening," continued Mr. Willoughby, *"the Boney Hand will be on display. Treat this sacred object with reverence and respect. Do not forget the curse that has been placed upon this hand!"*

The students solemnly nodded. All except for Charlie.

Curse? thought Charlie. What curse?

This was the stuff Charlie had been missing because of his limited sign language skills. Luckily, Mr. Willoughby explained.

"The legend tells us," signed Mr. Willoughby with even more drama and grandeur, *"that death shall fall upon anyone who dares to touch the Boney Hand!"*

Wait.

Death?

You'll DIE if you touch the Boney Hand? Really?

But Charlie hadn't thought this just inside his head. Without meaning to he had also stood up and signed *"death"* and *"really?"*

Every student stared at Charlie in astonishment. Even Frog.

"It IS real, Charlie!" signed Wendell. *"It is!"*

No one was laughing or kidding around. Not even Rupert. Charlie wished he would sink into the floor and disappear.

"You may take it lightly," Mr. Willoughby's signs spit at Charlie as Boris interpreted, *"but I can assure you we do not. Nor does the Boney Hand."*

With a scathing look at Charlie, Mr. Willoughby signed, *"Look over your lines and limber up your hands, while I limber up my voice."*

Then, sticking one finger in each ear, Mr. Willoughby closed his eyes and began practicing musical scales.

"La-la-la-LA-la-la-la," sang Mr. Willoughby. Charlie winced. Wendell and Jasper, who were both hard of hearing, winced as well.

Charlie standing and signing seemed to have shocked Frog back to herself. She looked at Charlie with concern.

"Wow," Frog signed as Boris quietly interpreted, *"I have never seen anyone doubt the curse of the Boney Hand before."*

"I wasn't doubting!" whispered Charlie, so Mr. Willoughby wouldn't hear him. "Honest, I wasn't. Death just seems kind of harsh for touching something, that's all!"

Rupert waved to get Charlie's attention. Most of the kids were also watching.

"If you don't believe in the curse," signed Rupert as Boris interpreted, *"then I dare you to touch the Boney Hand tonight!"*

"Double dare," added Jasper.

Rupert was twisting around what Charlie had signed.

"I never said I don't believe in the curse!" Charlie whispered as Boris signed for him.

Students shook their heads. Some signed, *"Don't do it, Charlie! Don't ever touch the hand!"*

"I never said I don't believe in the curse!" Charlie repeated. To Boris he said, "Make sure you sign 'I never said'!"

"Got you covered," said Boris.

"*I don't think he believes it,*" signed Rupert to the other students.

"*Ignore him,*" Frog told Charlie, dismissing Rupert with a twist of her hand. "*You need to practice your lines.*"

Rupert glanced at Mr. Willoughby to make sure his eyes were still closed.

Then he did something awful.

"*Cute!*" Rupert signed to Frog. "*You're so cute!*"

Frog stiffened.

"*No!*" signed Charlie. If Frog started a fight, Mr. Willoughby would side with Rupert. Adults always believed Rupert. He just looked so nice. Too nice to ever be mean.

"*Frog is so cute!*" signed Rupert.

Frog crumpled her script in her fists.

"*Such a cute little girl!*" he added.

Frog stood. Charlie and Ruthella grabbed her arms and pulled her back down just as Mr. Willoughby opened his eyes.

Rupert sat like an angel, his hands neatly folded in his lap.

Stealth bully.

Charlie could feel the fury inside Frog as he sat next to her.

"*Everyone stand up front,*" ordered Mr. Willoughby. Not everyone had seen that Mr. Willoughby was done practicing and was signing to them again. Students tapped each other on the shoulder and waved their hands to let each other know that rehearsal was starting.

"*Leave your scripts!*" ordered Mr. Willoughby as Boris interpreted. "*You should have them memorized by now!*"

Since he was in a church, Charlie prayed. He prayed he would remember all of his lines and that Frog would stay calm.

Mr. Willoughby adjusted his pirate hat to a flattering angle.

"*Remember,*" signed Mr. Willoughby, "*when I point to you, it is your turn to sign your part.*"

Mr. Willoughby took a deep breath and pointed to Frog.

"Pirates!" he began speaking. "Pirates once sailed the Hudson River—"

But Frog didn't sign because Rupert and Jasper were teasing her in the stealthiest way possible:

"*Frog is cute! So very, VERY cute!*"

Frog lunged.

Charlie and Ruthella lunged, too. They caught Frog around her waist before she could pummel Rupert and Jasper.

Mr. Willoughby stopped his recitation. "*What's going on?!*" he signed.

Looking angelic and afraid, Rupert pointed at Frog.

Frog kicked her legs and tried to break Charlie and Ruthella's hold on her.

Mr. Willoughby towered over Frog.

"ENOUGH!" he signed. Frog stopped kicking.

Charlie and Ruthella let go.

Frog lunged again.

They caught her once more.

"Out!" Mr. Willoughby screamed with his hands. *"NOW!"*

Frog shook off Charlie and Ruthella and stomped out of the church.

Charlie was alone after all.

7. Ready

Every Castle School for the Deaf student had at least one job, and one of Charlie's was to help Obie in the barn.

Because Obie was DeafBlind, he couldn't see people walking by and start up a conversation. So even when Charlie didn't have to work, he often stopped in just to say hello to Obie.

Charlie loved the barn. He loved the smell of hay and horses. He even loved the smell of manure, though Charlie would never admit that to anyone. Somehow the mix of all those smells was just right.

But today not even barn smell could cheer him up.

Charlie had failed at rehearsal. He completely forgot his lines once Frog had left the church. He couldn't even remember how to fingerspell. And the more everyone tried to help Charlie with his lines, the more confused he became until finally Mr. Willoughby had Rupert sign his part.

Rupert.

Charlie was dreading tonight.

When he walked into the barn, Darius, Obie's Deaf coworker and sometimes interpreter, was hammering a loose board into place. Obie swept the floor as one of the goats tugged on his pant leg. Max was napping in a pile of straw. Charlie stamped his foot on the wooden floor to let them know he was here.

Max sat up. When Max saw it was Charlie, he settled back down but kept his eyes on Obie. Darius stopped hammering and went over to Obie, touching his shoulder. Obie lifted his hands. Darius placed his hands underneath and signed that Charlie was here to work.

Darius sometimes used his voice, and he could even hear Charlie if Charlie was looking right at him and it wasn't too noisy. Obie told Charlie what barn chores needed to be done as Darius interpreted.

Charlie slipped his hands under Obie's bigger ones. "*Okay*," he signed. "*I will.*"

As Charlie went to get the pitchfork, Obie stopped him.

"What's wrong?" he asked.

Charlie put his hands under Obie's again.

"How," signed Charlie, *"did you know something is wrong?"*

"It was how you signed," Obie told him. *"I can feel it in your hands."*

As Darius interpreted, Charlie told Obie what happened last night on Vince Vinelli's show. He explained how upset Frog had been this morning and how Rupert wouldn't stop teasing her.

"But all Mr. Willoughby saw was Frog starting a fight!" said Charlie as Darius signed. "He missed everything that happened before that! And now Frog isn't allowed to be in tonight's performance."

"Which means Frog won't be there for you," signed Obie.

"That," signed Charlie. That was exactly it.

"What's Rupert like?" asked Obie. *"I don't know him very well yet."*

Rupert had only started at Castle School for the Deaf last year.

"Rupert? He's mean," said Charlie as Darius signed. "But he's mean in a way that sneaks up on you. When I first met him he was really nice to me. And then he—he changed! And I realized he's really a mean person who just looks nice. He's always misunderstanding what I sign on purpose, like this morning, when he told everyone I didn't believe in the curse."

"*I wonder why?*" signed Obie. Above his milky-blue eyes, his white eyebrows furrowed.

"*Why what?*" signed Charlie.

"*Why is he so mean?*" signed Obie.

"*I don't know why. He's just mean!*" Charlie couldn't spend any more time thinking about Rupert.

"*I'm worried about tonight,*" Charlie slowly signed to Obie. "*I don't want to mess up.*"

Charlie fingerspelled MESS UP as he didn't know how to sign it. Obie showed him the sign.

"*I wish I could be there for you,*" signed Obie. "*But caretakers haven't gone into the graveyard under a full moon since Boney Jack scared Silas P. Frankfurter to death a hundred and fifty years ago.*"

"Do you believe the Legend of the Boney Hand is true?" Charlie asked as Darius interpreted.

"*Let's just say I don't disbelieve it,*" signed Obie. "*Stories are powerful things. They can get inside of you and stay there, and no logic or reasoning can get those stories out of your head. Besides,*" Obie added, "*it's a bony hand crawling around with a death curse!*" Obie shivered. "*I don't want it to be true, but is it true? As the legend says—nobody knows.*"

• • •

By six thirty, visitors were pouring onto the castle grounds, jack-o'-lanterns shone in the darkness, and the scent of popcorn and hot cider filled the air. Around the bonfire overlooking the Hudson River, ghost stories were shared. Visitors toured the elaborately decorated castle. Kids bobbed for apples and made scarecrows.

Lanterns lined the pathway to the graveyard church, and inside the church, they lined the windowsills.

Charlie stood at the front of the church in a semicircle with the other students, all wearing their green-and-gold school shirts, waiting to perform. They were gathered around a dome-shaped object that was covered with a cloth and perched on a pedestal—the Boney Hand, waiting to be revealed.

A screen covered the front wall of the church, ready to display Boris's time-lapse film of the rising full moon. A restless crowd paced around outside, anxious to see and hear the legend.

Wendell stared at the covered Boney Hand with shining eyes. Charlie might have enjoyed the excitement of seeing a real bony hand for the first time—except he was about to throw up. And Charlie could not throw up. He had to do well. He had to sign his part.

Without Frog.

Charlie's hands were sweating.

He wiped them on his jeans and practiced his lines once more. Next to him was Ruthella. Behind him stood Boris, who was there to interpret student conversations as Mr. Willoughby once again did his vocal exercises with his eyes closed. When the performance began, Boris would sit down in the audience.

Ruthella looked happy, which surprised Charlie because Ruthella usually looked grouchy if she didn't have a book in her hand.

"There's a new time travel book," explained Ruthella as Boris interpreted, *"about Laura Bridgman and Helen Keller that I've been desperate to read. And then someone"*—Ruthella glanced meaningfully at Wendell, who was blushing and trying not to look at her—*"left that exact book in front of my dorm room, with a bow on it! I love this time of year when Boney Jack does his secret good deeds!"*

Suddenly, Ruthella noticed how nervous Charlie was. She patted his arm.

"I'll do my best to help you if you forget," signed Ruthella. *"It's just that I might forget, too, because I'll be thinking about my new book. But if you help me, I'll help you!"*

On the other side of the semicircle, Rupert signed and laughed with some students. But not Jasper. Jasper seemed to be deep in thought.

Rupert caught Charlie staring at him. He smirked at Charlie and signed, *"Cute!"* before returning to his poking and laughing.

The complete unfairness of Rupert being here and Frog not made Charlie want to lunge and pummel Rupert himself. Charlie willed himself to ignore Rupert and focus on not throwing up instead.

Mr. Willoughby finished his last vocal scale and opened his eyes.

"Ready," Mr. Willoughby signed by making the letter *R* with both hands and shaking them slightly. It wasn't a question; it was a command.

Boris sat down in the pews. Mr. Willoughby nodded to the student in the back of the church to open the doors. Visitors flowed in, talking and signing and pointing to the pedestal. Frog had told Charlie that many of the visitors were descendants of Jeremiah Bone, aka Boney Jack, just like Mr. Willoughby. Mrs. Castle was there, welcoming visitors. Chief Paley walked in, a head taller than everyone else. Charlie saw her try to sign with a few people.

DeafBlind visitors sat up front, each with a Deaf interpreter. They would experience the performance through their interpreters' hands.

Charlie spotted Grandma and Grandpa Tickler, along with Yvette. Charlie had never seen his grandparents on this side of the Hudson River. He couldn't believe they rode the gondola just to see him in tonight's performance. His grandparents were wide-eyed as they looked around the church. They spotted Charlie and gave him a thumbs-up. Yvette gave Charlie a crisp nod, which Charlie knew meant, "You can do this."

Thelonious Bone was the last person to file in. He sat in the very last row.

Mr. Willoughby faced the students and signed small, tight signs in front of his body so the audience could not see them.

"Do not," warned Mr. Willoughby, *"embarrass me."*

Charlie's stomach pitched.

Then Mr. Willoughby whipped around to face the audience, doffed his pirate cap, and bowed.

"Pirates!" Mr. Willoughby spoke in a booming voice as Rupert signed Frog's part with ease. "Yes! Pirates once roamed the Hudson River—pillaging villages, plundering farmhouses! But one pirate was different."

And so the Legend of the Boney Hand unfolded through the hands of the students and the voice of Mr. Willoughby.

The audience nodded along. The hearing people chimed in with a "That's right" or an "Mmm-hmm." The Deaf people signed and smiled their approval as the students performed their parts of this familiar story.

Charlie realized something. The audience *wanted* them to do well. His stomach settled just a little. Charlie glanced over his shoulder. He could see the full moon rising on the screen, with wispy clouds floating across its face.

Mr. Willoughby pointed to Ruthella. Ruthella just stood there, probably thinking of her new book she wanted to be reading. Charlie poked her with his elbow.

"The body of Boney Jack lay at the bottom of the Hudson

River," Ruthella signed as Mr. Willoughby recited. *"The fishes found him. They nibbled away until there were only bones. But Boney Jack wasn't finished. He had a message he needed to share. And this is what he used to tell that message!"*

The audience eagerly leaned forward.

Mr. Willoughby yanked off the velvet cloth. Under a glass dome, the Boney Hand rested on a red velvet pillow. Its yellow-brown bony fingers were curled, as if ready to pounce. The moon had risen to the top of the screen and now shone directly on the hand, illuminating its splendid horror.

Everyone shivered with delight.

"The Boney Hand," Wendell signed proudly as Mr. Willoughby spoke, *"made its way along the bed of the muddy river. It reached the bottom of the bluff and began crawling its way to the top."*

It was getting closer and closer to Charlie's part, but Charlie could only picture the Boney Hand crawling toward Castle School for the Deaf.

What were his lines?

What was he supposed to say?

The Boney Hand would soon reach the caretaker and deliver its message.

Mr. Willoughby would then point to Charlie. The whole audience would be waiting for him to sign what Mr. Willoughby narrated.

And he would just stand there and sign nothing.

It would be obvious Charlie didn't belong to this school.

Charlie's stomach roiled.

The church door opened. Frog slipped in and leaned against the door. All at once, Charlie felt solid and sturdy again. Everything came into focus. Charlie clearly saw Jasper signing. Charlie clearly heard Mr. Willoughby speaking.

"The caretaker," they signed and spoke, *"found the Boney Hand crouched on the church floor. He reached for it. The hand moved its fingers, and this is what it spelled..."*

In the back of the church Frog began to finger-spell. Along with Frog, Charlie slowly fingerspelled, NO...ONE...SAW...

And then Charlie perfectly signed, *"Saw what? Nobody knows!"*

The audience nodded.

"That's right," they murmured and signed. *"Nobody knows."*

Charlie, with Frog coaching him, had done it. He grinned as he heard Grandma Tickler say, "That's my grandson!"

• • •

Charlie hadn't realized how nervous the other students had been until he saw how happy they were now.

Everyone hugged and told one another how well they had done.

Except Jasper.

He stood alone, not participating in the back slapping and congratulating.

"You did it!" Ruthella signed to Charlie.

"You did it!" signed Charlie right back.

He turned to Wendell. *"Good job!"* he signed.

"Thanks," signed Wendell. *"I thought I was going to throw up!"*

"Me, too!" signed Charlie.

Wendell started to say something else, but then Frog and Boris were pushing in past him.

"Perfect!" signed Frog. She hugged Charlie. He felt so happy his heart almost hurt.

Audience members came up to the students. Chief Paley shook Charlie's hand. "Charlie, your signing was subtle yet full of nuance."

Chief Paley, who was also a writer, often used words that went over Charlie's head.

"Thanks," said Charlie. "I think."

Grandma and Grandpa Tickler made their way through the crowd along with Yvette.

"You did good," said Yvette when she reached him. "Your parents should have been here."

"Yes," said Grandma Tickler. "Myra and Alistair

should have been here watching Charlie, not watching Texas blind salamanders!"

"Ayuh!" said Grandpa Tickler.

"It's okay," said Charlie. "I'm glad you came, though!"

"We are, too!" said Grandma. "Now, why wasn't Frog in the performance?"

Grandma Tickler looked over at Frog, who was watching this exchange as Boris interpreted. Frog tossed her head and crossed her arms. She did not want to talk about it.

"I'll tell you later," said Charlie.

"We better get going," said Grandma, "or we'll miss the *Vince Vinelli Special Edition!* that's on tonight. Let's go ride the gondola, Irving!"

"Chief Paley said she'll ride back with you and walk you home," Yvette told Charlie before following his grandparents out of the church.

Mrs. Castle pushed through the crowd to Charlie.

"*I knew you could do it!*" she told him.

"*Frog helped me,*" he signed.

Mrs. Castle frowned at Frog, who wouldn't look at her mother.

"*I told Frog,*" signed Mrs. Castle, "*that she could come and support you. But once the Fall Extravaganza is over, there will be consequences for what happened.*"

"It wasn't Frog's fault!" Charlie tried to sign. But Mrs. Castle had turned away.

"Congratulations, Charlie!" Frog's father, who was hard of hearing, said. "You know, this reminds me of my own theatrical experience when I was a child—"

Mr. Castle switched to ASL, telling Charlie a story of when he was in a school play. As Boris dutifully interpreted, Frog's grandfather came over to Charlie. Grandpa Sol leaned over and gave Charlie's shoulder a gentle squeeze. He did the same to Frog before congratulating other students as well.

As Charlie watched Frog, his heart definitely hurt.

8. Chocolate

Charlie and Frog were the last students to leave the church. As they stepped outside, Charlie smelled the bonfire burning.

Do you want to go make s'mores, wrote Charlie, *before the next performance?*

Frog shook her head.

"*But they have chocolate in them!*" signed Charlie, making the letter *C* and circling it on the back of his other hand. Charlie could sign this because Frog had made sure he knew the sign for "*chocolate.*" It was one of her "*kiss-fist,*" or most favorite, things.

Frog shook her head again.

It was too soon, even for chocolate.

Frog was in a bad way if it was too soon for chocolate. Once again, Charlie did the only thing he could do.

"I'm sorry," he signed to Frog. *"I'm sorry about Vince Vinelli, and I'm sorry you're in trouble. It's not fair."*

Charlie fingerspelled FAIR, as he didn't know how to sign it. Frog showed him the sign and then gazed up at the starry sky.

"It doesn't matter," she told Charlie.

It doesn't matter?

Frog never signed *"It doesn't matter."* Everything mattered to Frog!

This wasn't good.

About Vince Vinelli and the letter, wrote Charlie. *I think you should write again—*

Frog stopped him and took his pen.

Let's face it, she wrote, *I'm not a real detective. I never really was. I've only solved one case, and I can't even talk about it. Maybe I'm meant to be a chemist. Or a clock maker.* Frog sighed deeply before she wrote, *Or maybe I'll make pies like Oliver.*

What was Frog talking about?

YOU ARE A DETECTIVE, wrote Charlie in big, strong letters.

"*No*," signed Frog. Then she wrote, *Sometimes dreams die.*

Frog stared out into the graveyard. *I need to be alone with my muse*, she wrote, *and accept this death.*

Frog thrust the notebook and pen back into Charlie's hands. She wandered down the path to D. J. McKinnon's grave. Only Frog would be fine sitting alone in the dark by a headstone.

A tour group entered the cemetery, led by a senior student carrying one of the lanterns. He pointed to the church. The windows glowed. Several visitors signed "*Beautiful*" before the guide continued walking.

Charlie decided to let Frog have a few moments alone. Then he would find her and cheer her up, even if she didn't want to be cheered up. He would just have to make her see he was right. She had to write to Vince Vinelli again.

"Charlie?"

It was Mr. Willoughby, leaving the church. "I must reapply my theatrical makeup before the next performance," said Mr. Willoughby. "No one is allowed in the church until then. Will you stay out front until I come back?"

It wasn't a question; it was a command.

Charlie nodded.

"Don't let anyone inside," warned Mr. Willoughby.

"I won't," said Charlie.

He sat on the bench outside the church and breathed in the cool night air. Charlie felt disconcerted, a word he had learned from Chief Paley. On one hand, he felt sad because Frog was feeling so down. But on the other hand, he felt happy. This was his first Fall Extravaganza, his first telling of the Legend of the Boney Hand. And Charlie hadn't disappointed his school.

An owl hooted.

Charlie remembered this past summer when he and Frog and Oliver had explored the graveyard at night and an owl had frightened him. It dawned on Charlie that he was sitting alone in a graveyard. The sad and happy feelings slid over to let a scared feeling squeeze in between them.

Charlie understood why Obie wouldn't enter the cemetery, especially at this time of year. With the Boney Hand so near, it was extra spooky. The moon shone above the trees, looking as round and full as it had last night when Boris captured its rising. Charlie heard Rupert's laugh on the other side of the graveyard wall. Hot anger welled up inside him as he thought about how unfairly Frog had been treated.

The tour guide's lantern flickered in the trees. Charlie hoped Mr. Willoughby would come back soon. How could Frog be back there alone? Mrs. Castle wouldn't approve. The tour group moved deeper into the cemetery.

The owl hooted again, and at that moment Charlie heard a soft thump from inside the church.

Charlie stood. He stared at the door, listening.

Where was Mr. Willoughby? Why wasn't he coming? He had told Charlie not to allow anyone in.

Mr. Willoughby had just left the church, so no one else *could* be inside. The only thing inside the church was . . . the Boney Hand.

Charlie's feet slowly moved toward the church door.

Why were his feet walking?

Why were his legs following his feet?

Why wasn't he running away?

Charlie told his feet and legs to stop.

They ignored him.

With a shaking hand, he reached for the iron door handle.

The sound of smashing glass from the other side of the door filled his ears.

Charlie's heart slammed against his chest.

The church door opened with a soft *creeeaaak*.

Charlie stepped inside.

At the front of the church, shattered glass covered the floor.

The Boney Hand teetered on the edge of the pedestal.

Then it leaped off the pedestal and onto the floor.

Charlie's mind screamed at his feet and legs: Run!

• • •

Charlie flew out of the church.

He bolted down the path, following the winding trail toward Frog, who was sitting with her back once again against D. J. McKinnon's headstone.

When Frog saw him, she jumped to her feet.

"What's wrong?" she signed. *"What happened?"*

Charlie didn't have the signs. He couldn't write. He could hardly breathe. He pointed toward the church.

"The Boney Hand!" he finally signed. *"The Boney Hand!"*

"What?" signed Frog. *"What about the Boney Hand?"*

Charlie grabbed her arm. *"Come on!"*

Together they raced to the door of the stone church, which was halfway open. Charlie pointed again. Then he shook his head and backed away.

Frog marched over to the entrance, flung open the door, and stepped inside. He heard her gasp and run up the aisle. Frog was running *toward* the Boney Hand!

Charlie couldn't let Frog be alone with it. He told his feet and legs to move. They obeyed.

He ran into the church and saw the reason Frog had gasped.

Charlie couldn't believe it.

It was true.

The legend was true.

The Boney Hand was alive and had crawled away.

The Boney Hand was *gone*.

Frog stared at Charlie. *"Where is it?"* she signed as Mr. Willoughby ran into the church, Rupert and Jasper right behind him. Mr. Willoughby shrieked when he saw the smashed glass and the empty red velvet pillow.

Then he turned his wrath upon Charlie and Frog.

9. Suspect

"He says he doesn't know what happened?" signed Mr. Willoughby. *"Of course he knows what happened! He was here!"*

Mr. Willoughby stood near the pedestal and the empty pillow along with Grandpa Sol and Mrs. Castle.

"Not now!" signed Mrs. Castle. *"He'll see you!"* Her worried eyes met Charlie's, who was sitting in a pew next to Boris.

"I don't care!"

Boris interpreted what they were saying. Only Boris was with Charlie, not Frog. Mr. Willoughby had insisted Charlie and Frog be questioned separately.

"Don't tell them anything!" Frog had whisper-signed to Charlie. Did Frog think Charlie had stolen the Boney Hand? But Frog was already being escorted out of the church.

Outside, Charlie could hear the crowd gathering for the next performance. Except there wouldn't be a next performance. Not without the Boney Hand.

"You know what this is like?" said Boris. "It's like that movie where the skeleton comes alive and starts, you know, attacking people."

"It didn't attack," said Charlie. "It leaped. It leaped onto the floor." Had it really done that? Charlie couldn't think clearly.

"I call that attacking," said Boris. "Wow. The Boney Hand is really alive. I wish I had had my camera set up in here to catch that."

"It can't be alive," said Charlie. "It's not possible."

"If it's not alive," asked Boris, "then how did it disappear?"

Grandpa Sol and Mrs. Castle approached Charlie and Boris while Mr. Willoughby glowered at the shards of glass on the floor.

"Tell us again what happened," signed Grandpa Sol as Boris interpreted.

"I heard a noise," signed Charlie, *"when I was sitting outside the church."*

"What kind of noise?" asked Mrs. Castle.

Charlie didn't know how to describe it. "It just sounded like someone was inside the church," said Charlie as Boris signed. "But then I heard smashing glass. When I opened the door, I saw the hand on the edge of the pedestal. And then the hand moved! It was on the table, and then it was on the floor."

Grandpa Sol's blue eyes were warm and steady. *"Are you sure?"* he asked.

"I think so," signed Charlie. *"I mean yes—I know it moved!"*

"You didn't see anyone enter the church or near the church?" asked Grandpa Sol.

"Just the tour group," said Charlie.

Chief Paley entered the building. "I did a walk around with Frog," said the chief as Boris signed, "to see if there was anything suspicious. And we searched the graveyard. Didn't find anything."

"Why was Frog with you?" Mr. Willoughby demanded. *"We haven't questioned her yet!"*

"She was outside. She asked if she could help," signed the chief. *"Is Frog a suspect?"*

"We have no suspects," signed Grandpa Sol. *"Yet."*

"I found a student who says he has something to add to the investigation," Chief Paley said as Boris signed. She went to the door and gestured to someone.

Rupert walked in.

"Excuse me for interrupting," Rupert politely signed

to the adults. *"I'm here because I need to apologize to every-one. Especially to Charlie."*

Rupert looked at him with earnest, honest eyes. Stealth bully.

"I did something without thinking at rehearsal," signed Rupert. *"I made a bad joke to Charlie, about touching the Boney Hand. He said he didn't believe in the curse, so I said, 'Why don't you touch it, then?' But it was a joke! I didn't think he would really do it! I'm really sorry, Charlie!"*

"I never said I didn't believe in the curse!" said Charlie as Boris signed.

"You were very flippant about it," signed Mr. Willoughby. Charlie saw him fingerspell the word "flippant."

"What does 'flippant' mean?" Charlie asked.

"It means you didn't take it seriously," said Chief Paley.

"I did!" signed Charlie.

"Did you or did you not say," signed Mr. Willoughby, *"that death seemed too harsh a punishment for touching the Boney Hand?"* Rupert must have told him Charlie had said that.

"I guess I did," said Charlie, "but I didn't mean to be . . . to be flipped or whatever that word is!"

"Flippant," said Chief Paley. "Synonyms include cheeky, glib, or saucy."

"I wasn't being—"

"Rupert saw you go into the church alone," signed Mr.

Willoughby, *"and promptly reported it to me. I was very clear no one was to enter the church until I came back!"*

"I was worried," Rupert said anxiously. *"I didn't want Charlie to take what I said seriously!"*

"I didn't!" said Charlie as Boris signed. "I heard something! That's why I went into the church. I thought someone was inside!"

Mr. Willoughby looked like his head was about to explode. *"Our Boney Hand—our precious Boney Hand—is missing! What will happen to our legend? What will happen to our yearly theatrical performance?"* Mr. Willoughby's signs grew larger and more dramatic, as if he were on a stage performing. *"We have a police officer here!"* he continued. *"We need to thoroughly search every student and visitor right now!"*

"This is not a criminal matter," signed Grandpa Sol. *"This is a school matter. We will deal with it."*

Mr. Willoughby threw his hands up in disgust and left the church. With a sly look to Charlie that only Charlie saw, Rupert followed.

"Charlie." Mrs. Castle put her hands gently on his shoulders before continuing to sign as Boris interpreted. *"You've been under a lot of pressure, what with learning a new language and being in the performance. Are you sure, are you absolutely sure, you didn't think that maybe it would be funny to try to touch the Boney Hand? And you broke the glass by mistake?"*

Charlie couldn't believe that Mrs. Castle thought he might have done it.

He felt like he was going to cry.

"*I didn't do it*," signed Charlie. But his signs had no power within them.

"*It's all right*," Mrs. Castle told him. But she didn't look like it was all right.

They left the church. Grandpa Sol, using Boris as the interpreter for the hearing people in the crowd, announced that the second performance of the Legend of the Boney Hand was canceled. The audience moaned.

Students gathered around and asked what happened to the Boney Hand. Grandpa Sol told them he would come to their dorm rooms tonight and talk to them after the Fall Extravaganza.

Frog was nowhere to be found.

As the students left, Charlie was given many backward glances. Boris interpreted what the kids were saying.

"*Rupert saw him go into the church alone!*"

"*Rupert said there was no reason for him to go in— Willoughby told him to stay outside!*"

"*Rupert saw the glass dome was smashed! It happened right after Charlie went inside!*"

"*Remember Rupert dared him? Rupert said he never thought Charlie would really do it!*"

Everything was "Rupert saw this" or "Rupert said that."

Rupert. The stealth bully.

Many students pointed at Charlie. Then they touched their index finger to the side of their forehead, palm facing down. They pulled their finger off their forehead twice, bending it each time.

Charlie asked Boris what that sign meant.

"Suspect," said Boris. "They suspect you stole the Boney Hand."

10. Please

Charlie waited with Oliver for the gondola. They watched Mr. Simple flash a message with his signal lamp, letting the castle know the gondola was starting its journey across the river. Charlie observed a single leaf falling from a tree, twirling and spinning alone in the air.

Frog was nowhere to be found.

Where had she gone?

What was she doing?

Did she think Charlie was guilty?

He watched students stream back to their dorms for the night. Wendell walked alone behind a group of kids.

Rupert was saying something to Jasper that made him hang his head.

Finally, Charlie said what he was sure Oliver was thinking.

"Everyone thinks I took it," said Charlie.

"Nah," said Oliver.

Charlie gave Oliver his best Frog look.

"Okay—maybe," he said. "What *did* you see? Did you really see the Boney Hand move?"

When Charlie had entered the church, the hand was on the edge of the pedestal. Had it pounced? Or had it fallen?

The Boney Hand was gone. He hadn't imagined that.

Charlie had to trust his own eyes.

"I saw it move," he said.

"For almost one hundred and fifty years," said Oliver, "the legend has been told—that the Boney Hand crawled up the cliff and fingerspelled to the caretaker." Oliver looked around. "Where do you suppose the hand is? It could be crawling around here right now. How am I going to sleep tonight?"

Obie was walking toward Charlie with one hand on Darius's shoulder and Max close at his side.

"What happened?" signed Obie.

With Darius signing, Charlie did his best to tell Obie what he saw and heard. He kept one hand resting lightly on Obie's forearm, letting Obie know he was still there and paying attention. Obie asked many questions. But most of Charlie's answers were *"I don't know."*

Because Charlie didn't know anything. He just knew the Boney Hand was gone.

"I'm sorry," he finally signed under Obie's hands.

"Why are you sorry?" asked Obie.

And once again Charlie answered, *"I don't know."*

As Obie and Darius walked away, Max pushed his body into the side of Obie's leg, the doggie version of the *"I'm-here-if-you-need-me"* sign. Charlie was sure Max was trained in many things, but he doubted he had been trained to protect his owner from a bony hand.

Millie and Bear bounded down the hill with Mrs. Castle and Chief Paley behind them.

But still no Frog.

Millie flung herself at Charlie. Bear licked his hand.

"I am never, ever going anywhere without Bear again," said Millie.

"You never do anyway," said Oliver.

"I do, too, Oliver!" said Millie. "But I'm not going to anymore because I don't want the Boney Hand to get me."

Mrs. Castle bent over and gave Charlie a hug, making the humming noise in her throat. Charlie felt the sound reverberate all the way through him. But Mrs. Castle didn't say, "I believe you."

"Bedtime!" she signed to Millie. Millie took her

mother's hand and followed her back to the castle. Bear trotted along beside them.

"Mrs. Castle had me call your grandparents and tell them the situation," the chief told Charlie. Her cell phone rang. "I love that technology works up here! Hello?" said the chief as she walked away.

Charlie and Oliver watched the gondola cross the Hudson River. It was colder now. The jack-o'-lantern candles had burned out. The bonfire lay smoldering. And a bony hand might be creeping around.

It had to be just a story.

And there had to be a logical explanation for what happened tonight. But just in case, Charlie lifted his feet and sat cross-legged on the bench. Oliver knew what he was thinking and did the same.

"Good idea," said Oliver, squinting at the ground. "You never know."

Just before the gondola reached the top of the bluff, Frog appeared in the castle doorway.

Something on her head glinted in the moonlight.

It was a tiara.

Frog was wearing a statement jewelry piece again. This made Charlie so happy that he almost forgot about the Boney Hand. He watched Frog run toward them. She asked Oliver to interpret for Charlie.

"What do you say?" asked Oliver.

"Please?" Frog rubbed a flat hand in a circle on her chest.

"Sure," he signed.

Frog faced Charlie. Her eyes gleamed like her tiara.

"This is our next case!" Frog told Charlie. *"We're going to investigate and solve this mystery! I'm going to prove to everyone that I am not cute—I'm a detective! Are you in? If you are, then meet me at ten a.m. tomorrow at the Castle-on-the-Hudson Museum."*

Of course.

That was it.

That's what they had to do. They had to find the Boney Hand themselves and prove that Charlie hadn't taken it. Frog, with Charlie's help, would find out what had really happened to the Boney Hand.

It was then Charlie realized Frog hadn't signed, *"We need to prove you're innocent!"*

Did that mean Frog also suspected Charlie? He was afraid to ask her that question. He wasn't sure he wanted to know the answer.

Besides, Frog was back.

"I'm in," signed Charlie.

11. Promise

That night, Charlie could hardly sleep.

He tossed and turned, tangling himself in his sheets and blankets as he dreamed.

Charlie was inside the church, staring at the Boney Hand under its glass dome. He watched the hand wedge its bony fingers under the glass. It tilted the dome up, up, up, until it toppled over and smashed to smithereens.

The Boney Hand began to crawl.

It inched down the pedestal and plopped on the stone floor.

It reared up on the heel of its palm. The tips of its fingers bent forward and stared at Charlie as if they had eyes. Suddenly, the fingertips dropped to the floor. The hand raced down the aisle toward Charlie, faster and faster until it jumped right on his—

Charlie bolted upright, breathing hard.

It's just a dream, he told himself. Just a dream.

Then Charlie remembered last night. He wished *that* had been just a dream. But—Charlie felt a sliver of hope—Frog was determined to solve the case. They were going to find out what really happened. He pulled on jeans and a T-shirt and headed downstairs.

Grandma and Grandpa Tickler were at the breakfast table, eating bowls of cereal. Yvette had not arrived yet. Sunday mornings Yvette went to church.

Grandma Tickler put down her spoon.

"We're ready, Charlie!" said Grandma. "We're ready to help you with the Boney Hand!"

"Help me?" Charlie's mind was fuzzy from lack of sleep. Chief Paley had told his grandparents everything that happened last night on the phone, and then repeated the story after she walked Charlie home. Charlie had chimed in, but he was so worn out after what happened he went straight to bed.

Except, of course, Charlie couldn't sleep.

"What do you mean, help me?" he asked.

"Help you solve the case!" said Grandma. "Our Vince Vinelli When Crime Is a Fact, Good People Act detective kit hasn't arrived yet, but we won't let that stop us!"

"Ayuh!" agreed Grandpa Tickler.

"No!" said Charlie without thinking.

His grandparents' faces fell.

Charlie had said "no" because he knew Frog wouldn't want Grandma and Grandpa involved. Charlie wasn't sure *he* wanted them involved. Except . . . wasn't this what Charlie had been wanting? For his grandparents to do something else besides watch television?

"I mean," said Charlie hastily, "*no* way when crime is a fact, good people won't act."

His grandparents' faces brightened.

"Exactly!" said Grandma. "We want to act! We want to solve a mystery!"

"Ayuh!"

Charlie had no idea how to get out of this.

"Because," said Charlie slowly as he tried to think of what to say, "you can't just sit by and do nothing . . . because good people do good things."

"And we," said Grandma Tickler, "are good people!"

"But!" Charlie added. "Good people first have to know where to start. That's why I am going to meet Frog this morning. Frog has a plan."

"Perfect," said Grandma, "we'll come with you!"

If Yvette were here, she would be watching Charlie with a look that said, "What are you going to say to that?"

Charlie suddenly knew what to say.

"You can't have too many detectives all together," said Charlie. "Otherwise criminals might get suspicious."

This made sense to Grandpa Tickler. "Ayuh," he said.

"If you say so, Charlie," said Grandma. "But we'll be waiting for you to let us know how we can help with the next step. You promise we can help, don't you?"

"I promise, Grandma," said Charlie.

In his mind, Charlie signed "*promise*" by touching the side of his index finger to his lips. Then he changed it to a flat hand and placed it on top of his fist.

Charlie would just have to convince Frog that involving his grandparents would help their investigation, not hinder it.

"I wonder what the next step will be!" said Grandma. "Don't you, Irving?"

"Ayuh."

"In the meantime, we'll have to find our own mystery to solve," decided Grandma.

"That's a great idea," said Charlie, surprised that he was relieved to avoid an outing with this new version of Grandma and Grandpa Tickler.

Because, for the first time, Charlie missed the E-Z-chair-recliner-TV-watching-Charlie-ignoring grandparents they had been when he first arrived at Castle-on-the-Hudson.

12. Who?

Although Charlie arrived before ten o'clock, Frog was already there, reading at a corner table.

The Castle-on–the-Hudson Museum was actually the Castle-on-the-Hudson Museum *and* Historical Society.

It was housed in what used to be the Castle-on-the-Hudson General Store. There was an old-fashioned cash register, old coffee makers and coffeepots, and glass jars full of licorice and lollipops that Charlie hoped were not old. Pictures of Castle-on-the-Hudson covered the walls. Miss Tweedy was dusting a framed photograph of a horse-and-carriage race on Main Street.

"Hi, Miss Tweedy," said Charlie. "So this is the Museum and Historical Society."

Miss Tweedy sniffed. "I prefer calling it just a museum, since I am only responsible for the museum part, which is all the stuff you can *see*." Miss Tweedy waved her duster around. "I make sure it remains dust-free. Cornelius van Dyke is in charge of the historical society part. That's all the stuff you can't see." Clearly Miss Tweedy did not think the historical society part was as important as the museum part.

"Can you believe it, Charlie?" said Miss Tweedy as she dusted the cash register. "The Boney Hand is loose! Thank goodness it's loose at the castle and not here. I told Thomas Cole he didn't have to be afraid, in case he was worried."

"Who's Thomas Cole?" asked Charlie.

"Thomas Cole is an artist who just moved to our village. A disheveled-looking man, always wearing paint-splattered clothes. Have you seen him around?"

Charlie remembered the man who entered the Flying Hands Café the morning of the Fall Extravaganza. He wore paint-splattered clothes.

"I think I saw him yesterday," said Charlie, "up at the castle." He remembered because Mrs. Castle had seemed anxious when she noticed him there.

"That's unfortunate," said Miss Tweedy.

"Why?" asked Charlie.

"Because," she said, "now Mr. Cole *does* have a reason to be afraid, if he plans to keep going up to the castle."

"Frog and I are going to find the Boney Hand," said Charlie.

"Frog already has a lead," said Miss Tweedy. She stopped dusting a coffeepot to give Charlie a meaning-ful look, which Charlie didn't understand but made him nervous.

"She does?" he said.

"Oh, yes," said Miss Tweedy. "Frog seemed to know exactly where to begin the investigation. She said it was the obvious place to start." Miss Tweedy stared long and hard at Charlie before saying, "Now if you'll excuse me, I need to visit Mr. Murphy."

And with that Miss Tweedy went through a door marked Employees Only.

Charlie knew when Miss Tweedy said "Mrs. Murphy," she meant "I'm going to the restroom." He wondered what "Mr. Murphy" meant?

And why had Miss Tweedy been looking at him that way? In a way that made Charlie feel guilty?

Miss Tweedy believed the Boney Hand was alive. Did she also believe that Charlie had stolen it?

And if Frog knew the obvious place to start, that could only mean one thing: Frog thought Charlie was the obvious suspect.

Charlie slowly made his way over to Frog. As he sat

down, Frog held up one finger to ask Charlie to wait until she finished reading the page in her book, *Pirates of the Hudson River*.

On Frog's T-shirt was a diamond daisy brooch, the fancy pin she'd been wearing the first time Charlie had met her in the Flying Hands Café. A few moments ago, Charlie would have been glad to see that brooch on Frog.

Now it just meant that Frog the detective was back. And Charlie was the one she was detecting.

Frog finished reading. She grabbed her pen and notebook. *I hope you didn't say the words "historical society" to Miss Tweedy,* wrote Frog. *She doesn't like sharing the museum with Cornelius and the Historical Society.*

"*I might have mentioned it,*" signed Charlie.

"*Well, don't!*" signed Frog.

Frog was definitely back.

Frog gestured to the books scattered on the table and wrote: *Miss Tweedy opened early for me so I could start my research.*

Charlie glanced at some of the book titles: *The History of Castle-on-the Hudson, The Tale of Boney Jack, Astoundingly True Ghost Stories of the Hudson Valley.*

"*I've been thinking,*" signed Frog.

Here it comes, thought Charlie.

Chief Paley and I found the church back door unlocked last night, wrote Frog. *Anyone had the MEANS to come in and steal the Boney Hand. So now we have to look at* OPPORTUNITY. *Everyone who attended the Fall Extravaganza had the opportunity to steal the hand, unless they have an alibi. So, we're left with* MOTIVE. *First, what would be a motive for an* ADULT *to steal the hand?*

Frog stopped writing and waited for Charlie to answer. But he couldn't think of any adults he knew who would steal the Boney Hand. Plus, there were hundreds of visitors there last night.

Frog studied him closely. Charlie wished he could think of someone so he wouldn't be the only suspect. But he couldn't.

Then, Frog continued, *I considered a kid. There were lots of kids there, but most of them were young kids with their parents. The older kids were mostly from Castle School for the Deaf. Right away I considered Rupert. He's a bully. Bullies do that type of thing.*

Charlie thought back to last night, when he had been sitting on the bench outside the church.

It couldn't be Rupert, wrote Charlie. *I heard his laugh outside the graveyard wall while I was waiting for Mr. Willoughby to come back.*

Frog tilted her head with a skeptical look. *I don't trust ears,* wrote Frog. *I trust eyes.*

I know Rupert's laugh, wrote Charlie. *It was definitely him.*

Frog sighed. *I loathe to admit it, but I have to agree. No CSD student would steal the Boney Hand. The curse is too powerful.*

Frog had obviously forgotten that Charlie had not taken the curse seriously enough yesterday.

Then I realized something, wrote Frog.

Nope. She hadn't forgotten.

Their detective partnership was over.

Maybe their friendship was over.

Frog would not be friends with a bony hand thief.

Frog stood and paced back and forth for a moment. Frog did her best thinking while pacing. She must be thinking how to tell Charlie she knew he was the thief. Frog stopped pacing.

It is a possibility, after all, she wrote.

Just say it, thought Charlie.

Frog paced some more and then she added: *I almost don't want to tell you because I know you'll say it's not true.*

Charlie took the pen from Frog.

I understand, wrote Charlie.

Really? wrote Frog. She seemed relieved.

Of course he understood. He would have thought he was guilty, too, if he were Frog.

Then you understand, wrote Frog, *why I was trying to find some corroboration.* Frog pointed to the books on the table.

Corroboration? What does that mean?

Chief Paley taught me that word, wrote Frog. *It means support for my theory.*

She gestured to the books again. *I found a few eye-witness accounts*, wrote Frog. *Men drinking ale at a tavern who swear they saw the Boney Hand crawling around. An old woman known as the village witch telling everyone the hand grabbed her throat. But nothing from a trustworthy source.*

Frog could see that Charlie had no idea what she was talking about.

I'm talking about my theory, wrote Frog, *that the Legend of the Boney Hand is TRUE! Let's make sure we're not overlooking the obvious, however hard it is to believe!*

Charlie felt relieved. Frog wasn't considering Charlie as the suspect. Then just as quickly, that relief turned to dread.

Because Charlie had *seen* the Boney Hand move. He knew he had. And the castle, just like the village, was a strange, odd place. So a hand crawling around just didn't seem that strange or odd. It seemed perfectly possible.

And *that* was scary.

I know where to start our investigation, wrote Frog.

"Where?" signed Charlie.

With someone, she wrote, *who will know for sure if the Boney Hand is alive or not.*

Charlie wasn't going to ask who because he knew Frog liked to keep things mysterious. But Frog kept waiting, so Charlie asked. He made the letter *L*. Then he put his thumb on his chin and curled his index finger up and down.

"*Who?*" signed Charlie, furrowing his eyebrows like Mrs. Castle had taught him.

"*You'll see,*" signed Frog mysteriously.

Just like Charlie knew she would.

13. Coffee

It was another crisp fall day in Castle-on-the-Hudson. Charlie saw many students in the village. Some students had part-time jobs, some students had internships, and some students went to the library. The villagers kept watchful eyes on the students, making sure they were well-behaved and reporting any trouble to Mr. Simple, who delivered the news to the other side of the river.

As Charlie and Frog walked, he remembered something. He took out his notebook and pen.

What about your consequences? he asked. Frog, after all, had nearly pummeled Rupert and Jasper.

Frog took the pen from Charlie.

It's thanks to you I have my freedom! she wrote. Frog steered Charlie around a bench he was about to run into before continuing to write.

Mom is worried about you and said I should keep you close. She said once the Boney Hand is found she'll deal with what happened.

Was Mrs. Castle really worried about Charlie? Or was she thinking Charlie stole the Boney Hand and it was smart to have Frog stay close to him in order to help Frog find it?

He saw Wendell Finch walking down the street. Charlie bet he was in the village to do another secret Boney Jack good deed. Charlie waved at him, but Wendell didn't give him his usual smile. Instead he bit his lip and shook his head before looking away.

Wendell loved the Boney Hand. He obviously believed the rumors that Charlie had taken it.

It wasn't me! Charlie wanted to yell. How many times could he say that? It seemed to make no difference. He had no power over what people believed about him. Just like no one believed Boney Jack wasn't a thief.

Charlie followed Frog across the street to Finkelstein's coffee shop.

Now he understood who they were going to see. Desdemona Finkelstein's fortune-telling business wasn't making much money at the moment. And she didn't want to go back to work as a lawyer. So Desdemona,

Fortune-Teller Extraordinaire, had been working for her parents.

As they entered the crowded shop, Frog inhaled deeply. She kissed her fist and then signed "*coffee*" by putting one fist on top of her other fist. She moved her top fist around in small circles as if grinding coffee beans.

Frog was coffee-crazy. She wasn't allowed to drink it, but she loved the smell of it.

Charlie and Frog sat down at the only empty table and watched Desdemona wait on customers. Desdemona was not a very good server.

She spilled coffee.

She forgot cream and sugar.

She gave a customer a sesame seed bagel instead of the cinnamon raisin one he'd ordered.

Finally, after all of her customers were served, Desdemona joined them at their table. She didn't ask what they wanted to order. She seemed to already know they needed a Fortune-Teller Extraordinaire.

"Debbie?" Mrs. Finkelstein called from behind the counter. Debbie was Desdemona's real name. "Why are you sitting down?"

"Just taking a quick break, Mother!" said Desdemona.

Mrs. Finkelstein frowned. "Five minutes, then." She glanced at Charlie, and her frown deepened. She crossed her arms and narrowed her eyes. First Miss Tweedy and now Mrs. Finkelstein? Why was everyone giving Charlie accusing looks?

Desdemona knew some ASL, so Frog very carefully signed to her what happened last night.

"It's gone?" signed Desdemona. *"The Boney Hand is gone?"*

Charlie would have thought a fortune-teller would have known this already, but he wasn't the lead investigator on this case. Frog took out her notebook.

In order to find the Boney Hand, wrote Frog, *we need to know the truth. Did the Boney Hand escape on its own or did someone steal it?*

Desdemona glanced at her mother, whose back was turned as she dried coffee cups. *I wish I had my Magic Black Ball*, wrote Desdemona. *But Mother doesn't allow me to bring it to work. I'll have to use something else.*

Desdemona tilted her head toward the other waitress behind the counter, who had been watching the three of them carefully.

That's Beryl, she wrote. *Beryl wants to be a fortune-teller too, someday.*

Desdemona laid a finger next to her nose. Beryl repeated the gesture.

Our secret signal, Desdemona told Charlie and Frog.

Beryl shot a nervous look at Mrs. Finkelstein before she took out the filter from the coffeepot. She put it on a plate, brought it over to them, and hurried back behind the counter.

Desdemona shook the coffee grounds onto the plate. Frog breathed in deeply and kissed her fist once more. Desdemona studied the coffee grounds. She stirred them around with her index finger. She peered even closer. Frog watched with rapt attention.

What could Desdemona possibly see? Because Charlie only saw coffee grounds.

Finally, Desdemona pushed the plate away.

"This isn't good," she signed.

"What isn't good?" asked Frog.

Charlie gripped the edge of the table with both hands. Did the coffee grounds see Charlie in the church with the Boney Hand? Could coffee grounds lie? Could coffee grounds tell Desdemona that Charlie was the thief?

Desdemona stared at the plate one more time.

"Oh, this is dreadful," signed Desdemona. *"Absolutely dreadful."*

"WHAT?" Charlie and Frog signed together.

The coffee grounds, wrote Desdemona, *REFUSE to tell me what they see.*

14. Work

"What do you mean 'the coffee grounds refuse to tell you'?" asked Frog.

Charlie couldn't believe this conversation. Coffee grounds don't talk! Coffee grounds don't know anything about a bony hand!

I mean, wrote Desdemona, *they are refusing to SHOW me what happened.*

"Debbie!" Mrs. Finkelstein called. Desdemona and Charlie looked over at her. Frog, seeing them both turn their heads, looked as well.

"Your break is over," said Mrs. Finkelstein. "There's work to do!"

So Frog would understand what she was saying, Mrs. Finkelstein pointed to Desdemona and signed "*work*" by making two fists. She tapped the bottom of one fist on the back of the other fist. *Work.*

"Yes, Mother," sighed Desdemona.

Mrs. Finkelstein scowled at Charlie before pouring a cup of coffee for a customer. Charlie looked at the floor. Frog tapped him on the shoulder and pointed to the notebook. Desdemona was writing again.

You and Charlie, she wrote, *are going to have to find out the truth on your own. Be careful.*

Be careful? Be careful of what? Charlie was going to ask, but Desdemona was already retying her apron.

"Waitressing," said Desdemona, "is so much harder than fortune-telling. Or lawyering," she added as she went back to work.

Frog reached for the pen.

Desdemona's right. We have to be careful.

"*Why?*" asked Charlie.

Because, wrote Frog, *we don't know if the Boney Hand is really alive or not. And it if is, and if the hand knows we're looking for it . . .*

What do you mean "if the hand knows we're looking for it"?

I mean we have to be careful, wrote Frog, *that the Boney Hand doesn't find us first and give us the death curse!*

106

"*Are you serious?*" asked Charlie.

Dead serious, wrote Frog. *Pun intended, ha-ha.*

How could Frog make a joke right now? This wasn't funny at all.

We can't do anything about the fact that the Boney Hand might be alive, wrote Frog. *Suppose it isn't? Suppose someone DID steal it. That's where we have to focus because that's the part we can do something about.*

Frog was right. But Charlie hoped—everything inside of him finger-crossed—that the Boney Hand wasn't alive.

We need to think, wrote Frog. She drummed her pen on the notebook. *Who could it be? Who could have stolen the Boney Hand?*

Outside of Finkelstein's, Charlie saw Rupert and Jasper. Rupert was politely talking to the shopkeeper next door, who had come outside to fill a water bowl for dogs. Rupert was great at talking to adults. Right now, he looked like a very nice person.

Rupert, the stealth bully.

He caught sight of Charlie and Frog watching him through the window. As the shopkeeper went back inside, Rupert made a face and signed *"cute"* to Frog and *"thief"* to Charlie. Jasper did the same.

Frog stood. Charlie yanked her back down.

Rupert and Jasper laughed and walked away.

Frog grabbed the pen. *I wish we could pin the theft on*

Rupert, wrote Frog. *If it wasn't for his alibi and the death curse, I would!*

Charlie wished they could, too.

"No student would ignore the death curse," added Frog, almost as if to convince herself. *Besides,* she wrote, *a detective has to be impartial. She can't let feelings influence a case.*

Frog meant she couldn't blame Rupert just because she didn't like him. Charlie tried to think who could be the most likely suspect.

Someone who wasn't Charlie.

Someone who was there last night.

Someone who—

Something outside caught Charlie's eye. It was Matilda, washing the big window of Blythe and Bone Bookshop across the street.

Bone. Thelonious Bone.

"What?" signed Frog. *"What is it?"*

Thelonious Bone, wrote Charlie, *was at the performance last night. Why would he come when Matilda said he hates seeing the Boney Hand being used that way?*

Are you sure you saw him there? asked Frog.

Charlie was sure.

Then we need to find out, she wrote, *why Bone would come all the way across the river to see something he hates.*

Frog tapped the pen to her lips. *Maybe,* she wrote, *Bone stole the Boney Hand so it would never be on display again. That would be a motive!*

But what about the death curse? wrote Charlie.

Maybe Bone is so old the thought of dying doesn't bother him, wrote Frog. *If he wants to ignore the death curse, that's his choice. He was there and he has a solid motive.*

"Okay," signed Charlie, *"but we need a plan."*

Charlie fingerspelled PLAN. Frog showed him how to sign it, and then asked: *"A plan for what?"*

"A plan," signed Charlie, *"for how we're going to talk to Bone."*

"I don't need a plan!" Frog signed slowly so Charlie would understand. *"He's a suspect. I'm going to question him!"*

"Remember what happened the last time?" asked Charlie.

Bone had been highly insulted when Frog questioned him about the death of Mr. Woo, the Castle-on-the-Hudson librarian. Even though Mr. Woo had been ninety-nine years old and had probably died of old age.

Frog remembered.

"Fine!" she signed. *"We'll talk to Matilda first and see what she can tell us. Then we'll figure out the next step."*

• • •

They crossed the street to Blythe and Bone Bookshop. Matilda paused her window washing and wiped her hands on her jeans.

"*I heard what happened!*" Matilda signed slowly for Charlie. "*Who would want to steal the Boney Hand?*"

"*That's why we wanted to talk to you,*" signed Frog.

"*I saw Bone last night,*" Charlie signed to Matilda.

"*Where?*" she asked.

"*In the church,*" signed Charlie, "*at the Legend of the Boney Hand.*"

"*Are you sure?*" she signed. "*Bone hates the legend. He would never watch it.*"

"*I'm sure,*" signed Charlie.

"*That's strange. But then, Bone has been acting strange lately.*" Matilda repeated what she signed for Charlie when she saw he didn't understand.

"*What do you mean 'acting strange'?*" asked Frog.

"*Just acting very mysterious. For instance, he's been disappearing every Sunday night at six twenty-five p.m. on the dot—for months now. But he won't tell me where he goes.*" Matilda repeated what she signed for Charlie.

"*Have you followed him?*" asked Frog.

"*No, I haven't followed him!*" signed Matilda. "*He's an adult! He has a right to privacy.*"

Matilda reached into the soapy bucket for her sponge and started washing the window again.

Frog took out her notebook.

We're coming back tonight, she told Charlie, *to follow Bone.*

15. Joking

Yvette was sweeping the front porch as Charlie and Frog walked up the steps.

"You don't want to go in there," she told them. For Frog, Yvette pointed to the house and shook her head.

"*What's wrong?*" Frog signed and Charlie spoke.

Yvette just swept the broom harder.

That was enough to give Charlie pause.

It had the opposite effect on Frog.

She strode right into the house. Charlie hurried in after her. Inside the front door was a bright red box with the words VINCE VINELLI, INC. EXPRESS DELIVERY on it.

The detective kit.

Uh-oh.

"Is that you, Charlie?" called Grandma. "We've been waiting for you!"

"Ayuh!"

Charlie and Frog walked into the living room. Grandma and Grandpa Tickler were not sitting in their E-Z chair recliners.

Grandma and Grandpa Tickler were standing in their pretend fighting stances and wearing the entire contents of their Vince Vinelli When Crime Is a Fact, Good People Act detective kit.

His grandparents each wore a black beanie hat, a fake mustache, a fanny pack with a pair of plastic hand-cuffs hanging off it, black gloves, black stretchy pants, and a black T-shirt that read *When Crime Is a Fact, Good People Act!*

They looked like cartoon criminals, not detectives.

Charlie was mortified.

Frog stared at them with her mouth wide open.

"Our detective kit arrived!" said Grandma. "We're ready to help solve the Mystery of the Disappearing Boney Hand! Tell Frog!"

"Ayuh!"

"Don't say 'tell Frog,'" Charlie said automatically. "Tell her yourself."

He handed his notebook and pen to Grandma.

Charlie had completely forgotten that his grandparents were waiting to help solve their first case. Just like he had forgotten Grandma ordered the Vince Vinelli When Crime Is a Fact, Good People Act detective kit.

If he had paid attention to what was inside the detective kit, he definitely would have remembered.

Frog read what Grandma had written. She raised an eyebrow to Charlie and signed, *"They're joking, right?"*

Frog made the ASL letter *X* with both hands, and put one on top of the other. Then she slid the top *X* forward over the bottom *X* twice. *Joking.*

Grandma and Grandpa Tickler were not joking.

Charlie had wanted them out of their E-Z chair recliners.

Now they were.

Charlie had wanted them to pay attention to him.

Now they were.

And Charlie had promised they could help.

"Just a minute, Grandma," said Charlie, taking back his notebook and pen. He pulled Frog to the side. Frog pulled out her own pen and notebook.

No way! wrote Frog. *They cannot help us solve this case!*

They want to be detectives, wrote Charlie. *Just like you do!*

They're not detectives! Frog scribbled in her notebook. *They've never solved a case before!*

Then let them solve their first case! Charlie scribbled back. *Or at least help us!*

They'll get in the way! wrote Frog.

I won't let them, Charlie promised. *We have to get our homework done this afternoon anyway. So how about they watch Bone until we go back to the bookshop?*

What for? asked Frog. *Bone doesn't leave until 6:25 p.m. Matilda said so!*

Just in case, wrote Charlie. *Herman can drive them. They can stay in his taxi and watch. If Bone leaves early, they can follow him.*

Frog raised an eyebrow as she watched Grandma Tickler help Grandpa Tickler reattach his mustache as he pulled his stretchy pants high above his waist. Frog gave Charlie her why-is-my-life-so-hard look.

It was a look Charlie knew well. He felt the same way.

Suppose, wrote Frog, *Bone sees them spying on him?*

They like lying down, wrote Charlie. *So I'll tell them to sit in the taxi like they would in their E-Z chair recliners! Bone won't see them.*

Frog sighed. But she didn't protest. Charlie took that as a yes.

Yvette packed a picnic lunch to sustain them. When Herman arrived, he beeped his horn. Charlie's grandparents got into the taxi, and Yvette put the lunch basket on the front seat next to Herman.

"Don't let anyone see you," said Charlie as he closed the taxi door.

"Right," said Grandma Tickler, "because we don't want the suspect to know we're following him."

"That, too," said Charlie.

• • •

Charlie and Frog spent the afternoon at the kitchen table, working on math and English. Just as they were ready to leave for Blythe and Bone Bookshop, the phone rang.

"Hello, Tickler residence," said Charlie.

"Darling, it's me—your mother!" said Mrs. Tickler.

"And me, your father!" said Mr. Tickler.

"Hi, Mom and Dad," he said.

"Oh, good! We can hear you," said Mrs. Tickler.

"Who?" signed Frog.

"My mom and dad," signed Charlie. Into the phone, he said, "How are the salamanders?"

"Texas blind salamanders," said Mr. Tickler.

"Oh, but they're not blind!" said Mrs. Tickler. "I mean they are, but not where it counts—because they *can* see—just not with their eyes."

"Cute little buggers are often ignored," said Mr. Tickler, "because they live in caves and are hidden from view."

"But they're right there!" said Mrs. Tickler. "You just have to look and you would see them, plain as day!"

"Indeed!" said Mr. Tickler.

"Now, Charlie," said his mother, "the reason we called is that we're concerned about you."

"You are?" said Charlie. He had never, ever heard his parents say that before.

"Yes, we are," said his father. "We called earlier today, but you weren't home. Your grandparents told us—"

"It was Yvette," corrected Mrs. Tickler.

"—Yvette told us we should be," said Mr. Tickler. "Concerned about you, that is. And so we are. She mentioned something about bones. It didn't sound good, did it, Myra?"

"No, it didn't, Alistair!"

"There's nothing to worry about!" said Charlie.

"Charlie is telling us not to be concerned, Myra," said Mr. Tickler. "Now we have a conundrum."

Conundrum. That was a Chief Paley word. It meant a dilemma or a problem. Maybe, Charlie thought, he should just talk to his parents. He had looked through a few of the library books his parents left behind. In one of them it said if a kid talks to his parents, and the parents listen, the kid can feel better.

"Okay," said Charlie. "Do you remember the Legend of the Boney Hand, up at Castle School for the Deaf?" Charlie's dad had grown up in Castle-on-the-Hudson.

"I do remember!" said his father. "Though my parents never took me to see it."

"Well," said Charlie, "the Boney Hand has been stolen."

"Stolen?" said Mrs. Tickler. "Is that why we should be concerned?"

"Yes," said Charlie, "because—" He took a deep breath. "Some people think I stole it."

"Why on earth would you steal a hand?" asked Mr. Tickler.

"I didn't!" he said.

"I should hope not!" said Mrs. Tickler. "Alistair, what do our parenting books say to do if your child steals?"

"I didn't steal the Boney Hand!"

But Charlie's parents weren't listening. They were looking for answers to Charlie somewhere else.

"That's a great question, Myra. Perhaps there's a chapter on thievery in one of those new books we bought here. Charlie, they have marvelous bookstores in Texas!"

Frog tapped her wrist. It was time to leave.

"Mom? Dad? I have to go," said Charlie.

"Well, all right," said Mrs. Tickler. "But be careful!"

"Yes," said Mr. Tickler, "be careful. Because we are— what are we again, Myra?"

"Concerned!" said his mother.

"Indeed, we are," said his father.

16. Shock

Herman's taxi was parked down the street from Blythe and Bone Bookshop. Grandma and Grandpa Tickler were asleep in the backseat. Herman was asleep in the front.

Some detectives! wrote Frog. *What if Bone left early?*

Now Frog was just being grumpy.

You said he wouldn't leave early! wrote Charlie. *Besides, it's only six o'clock.*

Charlie and Frog did not wake up his grandparents. Instead, they sat on a bench by the taxi and watched the front door of Blythe and Bone. It was already dusk. Lampposts were lit for the evening. Carved pumpkins glowed with candles, welcoming people into shops and cafés. Frog grabbed Charlie's arm.

"*My mom!*" she signed.

They slid off the bench and hid behind the taxi. Mrs. Castle would want to know what they were doing if she saw them. They leaned around the back of the car. Mrs. Castle was walking with the man in paint-splattered clothes—the man Charlie had seen yesterday at the castle.

"*Who's that?*" signed Frog.

I think he's the artist Miss Tweedy told me about, wrote Charlie. *He just moved to the village.*

Mrs. Castle and the artist crossed the street at the corner. Yesterday, Mrs. Castle had looked anxious when she had seen the man. But tonight she didn't seem anxious. Tonight she seemed almost relieved.

Frog nudged him and pointed at Blythe and Bone. Thelonious Bone was leaving the bookshop. He carried a briefcase. A briefcase that could easily hold a bony hand. Just then the taxi window rolled down. Grandma and Grandpa Tickler were awake.

"Charlie!" said Grandma. "There goes your suspect—get in!"

"Ayuh!" said Grandpa.

Frog, of course, didn't hear this. But she also didn't see this because she was already following Bone.

"No, Grandma and Grandpa!" said Charlie.

"What do you mean, 'no'?" demanded Grandma Tickler.

"I mean," said Charlie, "you already did your job! You staked out Blythe and Bone all afternoon! Now it's time for the next team of detectives to do their job."

"The B team, you mean," said Grandma. "Because Irving and I already decided we're the A team."

"Sure," said Charlie. "We'll let you know what happens. I have to go!" He hurried after Frog.

Herman started the taxi. He drove slowly, keeping pace with Charlie.

"Ayuh!" Grandpa Tickler called out the window.

"Irving has a good point, Charlie," said Grandma as the taxi rolled along next to him. "Isn't the B team the less experienced team? Shouldn't this be a job for the A team?"

Frog was at the end of the street. Bone had turned the corner. Frog opened her arms wide to Charlie in the universal gesture of "What in the world are you doing?"

"Grandma and Grandpa, please go home," begged Charlie. "I'll tell you everything when I get back!" He ran down the block and caught up with Frog.

Bone walked briskly, clutching his briefcase.

It was almost dark now. Charlie and Frog stayed in the shadows. Bone climbed the steps of a large Victorian house with a jack-o'-lantern out front.

Chief Paley's house, wrote Frog.

The first-floor windows were brightly lit. One of the windows was cracked open. Frog sidled up the porch steps. Charlie followed. They carefully peeked in the front window.

Miss Tweedy and Chief Paley were inside, along with Boris.

What was Boris doing here?

While Bone hung up his coat and hat, Miss Tweedy said to Boris, "We appreciate you coming. Although my American Sign Language is excellent of course."

That was completely untrue. Miss Tweedy knew a little ASL, but most often she tried to use Tweedy Sign Language, her own made-up form of communication. Frog was the only one who understood TSL.

"I'm still a novice signer," Chief Paley said to Boris, "though I try my best to utilize the language. You will keep everything you see and hear confidential, correct? Interpreters are supposed to keep everything confidential."

"We do," said Boris. "And I will."

"We discuss very personal things," added Miss Tweedy.

Charlie wrote everything they said as fast as he could for Frog. She was an expert at reading his messy shorthand writing. Charlie could see Frog had the same questions he had. What personal things? And why was Chief Paley worried about confidentiality?

"Something lovely happened to me at the library today," said Miss Tweedy. "I was the beneficiary of a Boney Jack good deed! Someone secretly left a gift-wrapped can of tuna fish for me and a rose for Mr. Dickens while I was visiting Mr. Murphy."

So that's why Wendell was in the village. Once again, Charlie wondered, what did "visiting Mr. Murphy" mean?

"You don't think," asked the chief, "that maybe the rose was for you and the tuna fish was for your cat?"

"Absolutely not!" said Miss Tweedy. "Everyone knows I adore tuna fish and that Mr. Dickens adores flowers!"

Bone came over with his briefcase and sat down next to Chief Paley. Bone seemed agitated. Miss Tweedy poured him a cup of tea and placed a cookie on the saucer.

"Thelonious, I can only stay a few minutes," said Miss Tweedy as Boris interpreted. "I told Enid I'd be home early. The Pig and Soap is full tonight! What with our bed-and-breakfast and my librarian duties and museum responsibilities, I have precious little time for my other passions!"

"We're all busy!" Bone snapped with his hands.

"There is no reason to be snippy with me, Thelonious!" Miss Tweedy said as Boris signed.

Bone took a sip of tea and put the cup down with a shaking hand.

"Elspeth's right," signed Chief Paley. *"There's no need to be peevish. This isn't easy. For any of us."*

"I can't do this anymore," signed Bone.

Was he confessing?

"Are you worried, Thelonious, what other people will think if they find out?" asked Miss Tweedy.

Bone sighed and nodded.

"It doesn't matter what anyone thinks," Chief Paley signed haltingly as Boris interpreted for Miss Tweedy. *"This is about you and your family history."*

Charlie and Frog gasped. Chief Paley *knew* that Thelonious Bone stole the Boney Hand? And she was okay with it?

"That's right," said Miss Tweedy. "And I can't wait to see it!"

And Miss Tweedy was not only fine with it—she also wanted to SEE the Boney Hand?!

If this wasn't enough, Bone said something even more awful.

"I'll show you," Bone told them, *"after I clean it up."* He pulled his briefcase onto his lap and held it tenderly.

Charlie and Frog gaped at each other. Just then car lights flashed and a horn beeped.

They spun around. The taxi was idling a few

houses away, his grandparents' faces pressed up against the glass.

"What's going on?" said Chief Paley. Charlie flattened himself against the side of the house, yanking Frog along with him. From the corner of his eye, he saw Chief Paley look out the front window. Grandma and Grandpa must have seen her too, because they ducked out of sight.

"It's just Herman," said the chief. "He must be waiting for someone." She turned away from the window. Charlie vaulted down the porch steps and ran over to the taxi.

"What are you doing?" whispered Charlie.

"Your suspect is in there!" said Grandma Tickler, pointing.

"I know!" said Charlie. "That's why Frog and I are here!"

"That's why we're here too!" said Grandma.

"Ayuh!" said Grandpa over her shoulder.

Charlie knew better than to argue. Instead he said, "Don't flash the lights or beep anymore, okay?"

Charlie raced back up the porch steps and rejoined Frog as she spied through the window.

"Well," Miss Tweedy was saying, "I wish I could discuss this more, but I have to get back."

She put on her wool coat and jammed a fuzzy hat on

her pink hair. As she left she said, "Thelonious, we stand by you. We're all in this together!"

Charlie and Frog scrambled off the porch and hid behind a bush as Miss Tweedy came out the front door. She turned left at the sidewalk, passing Herman's taxi. Grandma and Grandpa Tickler had already ducked down. Miss Tweedy gave Herman a wave.

Frog touched her forehead with her index finger. Then she brought both hands down in claw shapes.

"I'm shocked," signed Frog. *"Totally shocked."*

Knowing that Bone stole the Boney Hand wasn't that disturbing to Charlie. But knowing Chief Paley and Miss Tweedy approved of the thievery? Well, that changed how Charlie thought about every—

A piercing scream filled the air.

"Help!" shouted Miss Tweedy as she rushed down the sidewalk. "The Boney Hand just tried to grab me!"

17. Tree

Chief Paley and Boris ran outside as Charlie and Frog dashed to the sidewalk.

"*Tree!*" Miss Tweedy signed. She put her elbow on the back of her other hand. She spread the fingers of her raised hand, and twisted that hand back and forth.

"*What tree?*" signed Frog.

"There—over there!" Miss Tweedy gasped and pointed. "By Cornelius van Dyke's maple tree!"

Chief Paley ran down the sidewalk. Herman's taxi rolled down the street after her. Frog and Charlie started to run, too, but Miss Tweedy grabbed their arms.

"Don't leave me!" she cried. She was surprisingly strong.

Charlie and Frog helped Miss Tweedy sit on the bottom porch step. Bone walked down and handed Miss Tweedy his handkerchief. Then he hurried back up the porch. Miss Tweedy clutched the handkerchief to her heart.

"Death!" she sobbed as Boris signed. "Death nearly touched me!"

What did you see? signed Frog.

Thank goodness Miss Tweedy did not try to use Tweedy Sign Language. Instead, she allowed Boris to interpret for her.

"I saw the Boney Hand scuttling and scurrying toward me!" she said. "It was horrendous! It pointed its finger at me! Not the middle finger. That would have been even more horrendous!"

Charlie and Frog examined the ground by the bottom step. Boris and Miss Tweedy did the same. Without saying a word, all four of them stood and moved to the top step.

"Then what?" signed Frog.

"Then I screamed!" said Miss Tweedy. "And I ran!"

Miss Tweedy blew her nose into Bone's handkerchief and wiped it thoroughly. She clutched Frog's arm—thankfully not with the handkerchief hand.

"Do you realize what this means?" she asked as Boris signed.

Before Frog could answer, Miss Tweedy answered her own question in TSL. She jumped to her feet and swept her arms in the air. She tiptoed across the porch and squatted with one hand hovering over the floor. Finally, she performed a pirouette and three hops. Winded, she sat down.

Frog translated.

She says it means, wrote Frog, *that the Boney Hand either swam across the Hudson River or it rode over to the village on the gondola.*

How did Frog understand that? Charlie looked at Frog in amazement.

"Wouldn't Mr. Simple have noticed a bony hand riding his gondola?" Frog asked Miss Tweedy.

"Walter Simple," said Miss Tweedy, "wouldn't notice a bucket of bony hands riding his gondola!"

Chief Paley walked up as Herman's taxi returned.

"Did you find it?" asked Frog.

"I didn't see anything," signed Chief Paley. *"By the way, what are you two doing here?"*

Frog didn't answer the question. Instead she signed, *"Mom knows I'm in the village."*

Chief Paley turned her attention to the taxi. Grandma leaned out the window and Grandpa leaned over Grandma.

"Irma and Irving, what are you doing here?" Chief Paley called. Herman was asleep at the wheel again.

"We're with Charlie and Frog," said Grandma as Boris signed for Frog and Bone.

"Why are you incognito?"

"In cog what?"

"Wearing disguises."

"These are not disguises! These are our work clothes!"

"What kind of work?"

"Detective work!" said Grandma.

Charlie saw Frog shake her head ever so slightly. Grandma Tickler saw it, too.

"I want my lawyer," said Grandma. "That's what criminals always say on our favorite crime shows. But mind you, we aren't criminals!"

"Ayuh!" said Grandpa Tickler.

"Lawyers? Criminals? What are you talking about?" said Chief Paley.

But Grandma made a zipping motion across her lips.

"I'm disquieted and discomfited and yes, discombobulated by the idea of a bony hand on the loose," said the chief as Boris signed. She turned to Miss Tweedy. "Elspeth, will you give me a statement? Tell me what you saw?"

"This is horrendous," said Miss Tweedy as Chief

Paley led her inside. "Simply horrendous! I need to visit Mr. Murphy!" Bone followed them into the house.

Frog saw the question in Charlie's eyes. "*Visiting Mr. Murphy,*" she signed as Boris interpreted, "*means I need to take a nap.*"

"Charlie!" called Grandma as Boris signed. "Let's go search for the Boney Hand! Herman can drive us around the village. We have flashlights!"

Grandma Tickler shined her flashlight in their eyes as they stood on the porch.

"Grandma, we can't see!" said Charlie. "And I need to talk to Frog first."

Frog asked Boris a question. Boris shook his head.

"I told Frog I can interpret for a few more minutes," Boris told Charlie, "but then I have to go back in. And no, I won't tell Frog what the meeting with Chief Paley, Miss Tweedy, and Mr. Bone was about. Interpreters don't interpret and tell."

"*Well,*" signed Frog as Boris spoke, "*we're right back where we started. Either the Boney Hand is alive and scaring people, or a real person stole it and now is scaring people with it. But we have no idea who that person might be.*"

Frog paced on the porch. She paused for a moment to add, "*And I was so hoping it would be Bone! Now we need another suspect.*"

Just don't let it be me, thought Charlie.

But Charlie had left Frog for a few moments when they had spied on Bone to tell his grandparents to stop flashing their lights and beeping their horn. Did Frog think Charlie had been gone long enough for him to place the Boney Hand in Cornelius van Dyke's yard?

"If the hand is alive," signed Frog, *"then we have to be extra careful. The Boney Hand, as we just learned, could be anywhere."*

Frog went back to pacing.

While Frog paced, Boris said, "This is the coolest place—a village with no cell phone or Internet, lovable looney villagers, and a bony hand roaming around. But one thing is weird," Boris added thoughtfully.

"What?" asked Charlie as Frog continued to pace and think.

"You were there," said Boris, "when the Boney Hand first disappeared. Now you're here when the Boney Hand shows up again. Weird that it's always you."

18. Charlie

The next morning Charlie was bleary-eyed.

But not Grandma and Grandpa Tickler. Dressed in their detective outfits, they were playing cards at the kitchen table when Charlie came downstairs.

"Morning," said Yvette. "Heard you had an interesting time last night."

"It was an adventure!" said Grandma as Yvette served her scrambled eggs.

"Ayuh!" said Grandpa as he bit into his toast.

"Exciting is right, Irving!" said Grandma. "Charlie, we're ready to start searching again this morning."

Charlie cringed as he remembered driving around the village the night before. It had been Charlie's turn to lie low in his seat as his grandparents shined their flashlights out of the taxi windows in sweeping arcs, blinding villagers and visitors alike as Grandma shouted, "Anyone seen a hand?"

And then there was what Boris had said to Charlie. What had Boris meant by that? And why was Charlie feeling guilty when he had no reason to feel that way?

"I have school this morning," said Charlie as he sat down.

"We don't need the B team," said Grandma. "The A team has this case under control!"

"The A Team needs to eat their eggs before they get cold," said Yvette as she placed eggs and toast in front of Charlie. The eggs had bits and pieces of something unknown scrambled in with them. It didn't look good, but Yvette's cooking always tasted good.

"Thank you, Yvette," said Charlie. "What do you mean you have this case under control, Grandma?"

"Irving and I made a plan last night. First, we're going back to the scene of the crime, Cornelius van Dyke's maple tree. And then"—Grandma Tickler took a sip of milk—"we are going to make someone confess!"

Charlie stopped buttering his toast.

"Confess?" he said. "How?"

"We're going to pin the guilty person to the wall," said Grandma. "That's detective talk."

"Ayuh!"

"But," said Charlie, desperate to find some reasonableness this morning, "how would you even know if someone is guilty?"

"Oh, we can tell if someone is guilty," said Grandma, "by how that person looks!"

Yvette turned around from the sink. "How in the world can you do that, Irma?"

"We have eyes, Yvette!"

"Ayuh!"

"That's not how you really see someone," said Yvette.

"How else would you see someone?"

"You have to know them!" said Yvette.

"We don't have time for that, do we, Irving? We have a bony hand to find and a suspect to catch!"

"Grandma," said Charlie, "promise me you won't do anything until I get home. Please? For me?" Charlie gave her his best grandson smile, the one that he had seen TV grandsons give their TV grandparents when they wanted something.

Grandma and Grandpa looked at each other and then looked at Charlie. To Charlie's relief, they both nodded. As he ate his toast, he considered who could be his and Frog's next suspect.

They had to have a suspect.

The other options—Frog thinking Charlie was the main suspect or, even worse, that the Boney Hand was really alive—were unthinkable.

"While we're waiting for you," said Grandma, interrupting Charlie's thoughts, "Irving and I can work on solving our other mystery."

Charlie stopped eating. "What other mystery?"

"The Mystery of the Missing Remote Control!" said Grandma. "We woke up this morning and settled into our E-Z chair recliners, ready to watch all the terrible things happening in the world on our morning news program. I reached for the remote control, and it was gone! Irving had to get up and turn the TV on! And then, when I wanted to change the channel, he had to get up *again*!"

"Ayuh!" said Grandpa.

"It *was* awful, Irving," said Grandma. "Our first suspect, of course, was Yvette. But Yvette said—Yvette, what were your exact words?"

Yvette was wiping crumbs from the kitchen counter. Without turning around she said, "Why would I take your remote control?"

"That's exactly what she said," said Grandma. "So you're our next suspect, Charlie."

"I didn't take it," he said.

"Oh," said Grandma Tickler. "We were hoping for something more exciting than 'I didn't take it.'"

"I'm sorry," said Charlie. "But I didn't."

"Well"—Grandma Tickler brightened—"our next step will be to thoroughly search the premises."

Yvette shook her head as she put the milk back in the refrigerator.

"I'm sure you'll find it," said Charlie.

"Now that we have detective outfits," said Grandma Tickler, "you can bet we will!"

• • •

As Charlie sat in math class, he saw his name and Frog's name on the hands of other students.

Names were funny things, Charlie realized.

Why was Elspeth Tweedy called Miss Tweedy, yet her sister was called Enid? Why was Thelonious Bone just Bone instead of Mr. Bone or Thelonious? And yet Charlie could never think of Miss Tweedy as Elspeth or Enid as Miss Tweedy or Bone as Mr. Bone or Thelonious. Those names just wouldn't fit. Or take Desdemona. Her real name was Debbie. But why wasn't the name she chose for herself just as real as the name her mother and father had picked for her?

In ASL, instead of repeatedly fingerspelling someone's name, Deaf people often had name signs. Frog's name sign was one she had given herself at the age of three, when she chose the name Frog and the sign "*frog*" to go with it.

Frog had given Charlie his name sign. They had become friends because they decided to search for Aggie together. So Frog said Charlie's name sign would be based on the sign for "*search*," which was made with a *C* hand shape, the first letter in Charlie's name. But over time, his name sign became smaller simply because it was easier to sign. His name sign had finally settled to be the letter *C*, shaken slightly.

Now Charlie saw his name sign flying around the room. The signing was fast and furious. It stopped the minute Mr. Walth faced the class. It started up again once his back was turned. Everyone was talking about what had happened last night with the Boney Hand and how Charlie and Frog had been there. Charlie had no idea how everyone knew so quickly.

Charlie did not have an interpreter in class today. Miss Davenport was working elsewhere, and Mr. Willoughby had wanted to discuss something with Boris.

Rupert sat across from Charlie in the semicircle of desks. Frog and Jasper were in a different class. Charlie couldn't understand all the signing, but he understood the language of bullies.

He watched how Rupert would make a suggestion about Charlie and the Boney Hand. And then the other kids—not all, but most—would pick up the suggestion and stretch it like taffy, shaping it into a story about what happened.

Charlie could only catch pieces of Rupert's story. But he knew enough ASL that he could see Rupert was leading them to think Charlie was at the center of the mystery. And Rupert was signing something about Frog being connected, too. Many students still thought the Boney Hand could have disappeared on its own. But many of them believed Rupert's story about Charlie and Frog.

Charlie usually liked math because Mr. Walth made math interesting and fun, but today Charlie felt like his name sign: shaken.

Shaken loose. His connection to the school being pulled and stretched like a rubber band with each accusation and sidelong glance.

Until it would snap.

And he would no longer be attached.

"Charlie?" Mr. Walth held the dry erase marker out to him. *"Can you solve this problem?"*

Charlie shook his head. He had no idea how to begin.

19. A Hearing Person

Just before the end of class, a student came into Mr. Walth's room with a note for Charlie. Grandpa Sol, the superintendent of the school, wanted to see him in his study. Mr. Walth told Charlie he could leave. It was obvious Charlie wasn't able to think about math right now.

As Charlie walked through the quiet hallways that led to the superintendent's study, he knew why Grandpa Sol wanted to see him—it was because of last night and the Boney Hand.

Everything right now was about the Boney Hand. Charlie wished school to be like it was before the hand had disappeared. When he had felt—or almost felt—part of it.

He heard a faint knocking sound. He stopped and listened.

Tap-tap, pound . . . tap-pound-pound, tap-pound, tap-tap-tap . . . pound-pound, tap.

He couldn't tell where the sound was coming from. "Hello?" said Charlie.

Tap-tap, pound . . . tap-pound-pound, tap-pound, tap-tap-tap . . . pound-pound, tap.

Someone was deliberately knocking. He studied the closed doors up and down the hallway.

"Who's there?" he asked. Charlie felt silly for saying it. He was at a Deaf school where almost everyone was Deaf.

Tap-tap, pound . . . tap-pound-pound, tap-pound, tap-tap-tap . . . pound-pound, tap.

"Do you need help?" called Charlie. He tried a few doors, but they were locked. He still couldn't tell where the sound was coming from. But if someone was locked in somewhere, wouldn't Charlie just hear loud pounding instead of a repeated pattern of knocking?

Then the knocking stopped.

Charlie stayed still and listened.

He listened for a long time.

But there was nothing else to hear.

• • •

When Charlie arrived at the superintendent's study, he found Frog, Mrs. Castle, Boris, and Mr. Willoughby already there, along with Grandpa Sol. They were sitting in a semicircle on chairs next to the fireplace, where a cozy fire crackled and popped. An empty chair waited for Charlie. As he sat down, he caught Frog's eye. She shrugged and crossed her arms.

"*We asked you here,*" said Grandpa Sol as Boris interpreted, "*because we want to know what happened last night. Frog already told us what she saw.*"

"*We only knew to ask Frog,*" signed Mr. Willoughby, "*because Chief Paley told us!*"

"*I was going to tell you!*" signed Frog as her many silver bracelets jangled on her wrist. "*Chief Paley just beat me to it!*"

Frog crossed her arms again with a big huffy sigh.

"*Charlie, what did you see last night?*" signed Grandpa Sol.

"I didn't see anything." Charlie faltered as Boris interpreted. "I mean, I heard Miss Tweedy scream. And then I saw her running toward us."

"*What were you doing before you heard her scream?*" asked Grandpa Sol.

Charlie hesitated. He didn't look at Frog, but he knew

he couldn't lie. Especially not with Mrs. Castle there.

"Frog and I," Charlie signed slowly, *"were looking for Thelonious Bone."*

Thelonious Bone was a long name to fingerspell.

"Why were you looking for him?" signed Mr. Willoughby.

Frog interrupted before Charlie could answer.

"We want our lawyer!" demanded Frog, just like Grandma Tickler had said last night with Chief Paley.

"Lawyer?" Mr. Willoughby's left eye twitched.

"Yes!" signed Frog. *"Desdemona Finkelstein is my lawyer. And Charlie's. We're not answering any more questions until she's here. Right, Charlie?"*

"Uh . . ." said Charlie.

"This is ridiculous!" Mr. Willoughby slung his signs at everyone. *"SOMEONE stole an important piece of my—of our history! I have talked with the Board of Trustees. They agree with me—if it was a student who stole the Boney Hand"*—Mr. Willoughby looked right at Charlie and Frog—*"then that student will be expelled!"*

He stormed out of the office, slamming the door behind him. The sound reverberated through the wood floor and into Charlie's body. A log fell inside the fireplace, shooting sparks into the air.

"Edward Willoughby cares very deeply about the Boney Hand," signed Grandpa Sol to Charlie and Frog. *"It's*

part of his family's history as well as the school's history. He takes this very personally."

"And he thinks Charlie and I had something to do with it!" signed Frog, who was never afraid to say what everyone else might be thinking.

Grandpa Sol didn't say that Frog was wrong. Neither did Mrs. Castle. What was Mrs. Castle thinking? Did she think Charlie had something to do with the missing Boney Hand? He wished Mrs. Castle would say something. Anything.

But she didn't.

"Mr. Willoughby doesn't like me," added Frog.

"Or me," Charlie signed quietly.

Grandpa Sol didn't say either one wasn't true. He thought a moment before responding.

"Adults are only human," signed Grandpa Sol. *"Edward should control himself, regardless of how he feels. But, Frog, you challenge him. He often thinks you're disrespectful—"*

Grandpa Sol held up a hand as Frog started to protest.

"You're also a Castle, which holds its share of assumptions, fair or unfair. And, Charlie"—Grandpa Sol turned to him—*"in Mr. Willoughby's eyes, you are an outsider. Someone who hasn't yet earned the trust of the community. Someone who is still learning to sign. Someone who is hearing."*

"*But Mr. Willoughby is a hearing person, too!*" Frog signed "*hearing person*" by holding her index finger sideways in front of her lips and circling it outward twice.

"*With Deaf parents,*" added Grandpa Sol. "*That's a big difference. In a way, Mr. Willoughby feels protective of our community.*"

"*That's absurd,*" Mrs. Castle finally signed. "*We don't need protection!*"

"*I'm not saying it's rational. I'm saying it's emotional. His family, the Bones, have been part of our school for more than one hundred years.*"

Mrs. Castle stood. "*I need to get back to the café,*" she signed. "*That's the one good thing that has come from this—business is booming! It seems everyone knows what happened to the Boney Hand and now wants to come here and see the castle for themselves.*"

Mrs. Castle left the office. Frog signed something to Grandpa Sol, but Charlie wasn't watching anymore.

Instead, he thought about what Grandpa Sol had signed. The sign that Mrs. Castle saw but didn't say was the wrong sign to ever use with Charlie.

It played over and over again in Charlie's mind.

Outsider.

Outsider.

Outsider.

20. Stubborn

After school Frog wanted to get away from everyone, something she said was hard to do when everywhere you went you knew everyone. But the Castle-on-the-Hudson Museum (and Historical Society) was usually empty, with only Cornelius van Dyke there, or occasionally Miss Tweedy when dusting was needed.

Charlie sat across from Frog at a corner table. He tried to concentrate on his homework while Frog read another book about the Boney Hand, but he couldn't focus on math. He could only focus on being an outsider.

Cornelius van Dyke was reading and writing on a stool next to the old-fashioned cash register. Cornelius was helping Frog's father write a history of Castle School for the Deaf. Frog told Charlie that Cornelius didn't talk much unless it was about history. That was one of the reasons Frog liked coming here—no chitchat.

Charlie looked at the photographs on the wall. There was a picture of two people dressed in old-fashioned clothes, signing in front of the library. Charlie tried to figure out what sign the man in the bowler hat was making as he talked to the woman in the long dress. Finally he realized it was one of the first signs Frog had taught him—"*will*."

Maybe the man was telling the woman, "*I WILL get your book*" or "*I WILL come home as soon as I finish visiting the library.*"

Frog looked up. Charlie's hand dropped into his lap.

"*Why are you talking to yourself?*" asked Frog.

"*I'm not!*"

Frog started to open another book and then slammed it shut. She picked up her pen.

I feel stuck, wrote Frog, *because I don't know our next step. I can't find anything in these books that would help me figure out WHERE the Boney Hand would have crawled— if it's alive.*

"*We should probably search the graveyard,*" signed Charlie.

He was joking, of course. They should stay far away from the cemetery until the Boney Hand was found.

"*I've already been there*," signed Frog. "*Twice. Once in the day and once at night.*"

He asked Frog to repeat what she signed because he must have misunderstood her.

Frog did.

"*What? I was kidding!*" signed Charlie. "*What about the death curse?*"

"*I'm a detective.*" Frog slowed her signing for Charlie. "*I do what I have to do. I wanted to make sure the hand wasn't there.*"

She paused and then signed, "*You know what Rupert is saying, don't you?*"

Charlie had a vague idea, but he didn't know for sure because of his limited ASL. Frog picked up her pen again.

Rupert is telling everyone that you stole the Boney Hand for me so that I would have a real crime to solve. He said that I convinced you to do it once I knew you didn't care about the death curse. Because I want to prove I'm a real detective.

That's what everyone was signing in math class? Charlie knew it was bad. He just didn't know how bad.

Frog put her head down on the table. Her shoulders lifted and then dropped as she let out a heavy sigh.

Charlie had a horrible thought. Maybe Frog *had* stolen the Boney Hand just to have a crime to solve. She had been devastated after what Vince Vinelli said about her on national television. Finding the hand would redeem Frog. Make her the hero of the school.

Immediately, Charlie felt ashamed for even thinking this.

Charlie knew who Frog was on the inside. Frog was a great detective. She didn't want to solve a made-up case. She wanted to solve a real case.

As if Frog could read his mind, she sat up.

"Remember what Chief Paley calls me?" asked Frog.

Chief Paley called Frog tenacious. Frog's mother preferred another word— "stubborn." But both words meant the same thing: Frog didn't give up.

Charlie put his thumb on the side of his forehead, his fingers together, pointing up. Then he bent his fingers forward. *Stubborn.*

That's right, wrote Frog. *I'm tenacious. I'm stubborn. I don't give up. I am going to solve this case. No matter what it takes.*

21. Right

Millie was pouting.

Every time she threw the ball, Bear brought it back, but he brought it back to Boris. Boris finally stood and played ball with Bear, taking pictures of the huge black dog as he ran and fetched.

Tuesday was a bright sunny day, so Mrs. Castle asked the head cook to pack lunches for the students to eat outside. Some students refused to sit on the ground with the Boney Hand still missing. But it was such a beautiful fall day, it was hard to imagine the Boney Hand coming after anyone. Besides, at least in the daylight you could see it coming.

Charlie sat on a blanket with Millie, Frog, Oliver, and Ruthella, who was reading her new book while eating her peanut-butter-and-jelly sandwich.

"*It's just because Boris is new,*" signed Charlie, trying to cheer up Millie. "*That's why Bear is playing with him, instead of you. Bear played a lot with me when I first came here. But Bear loves you best.*"

"*Well, I'm not going to give Bear any!*" signed Millie.

"*Any of what?*" asked Frog. Today she wore a multi-strand pearl necklace as her statement piece. It looked like something a rich old lady would wear to a tea party. But Frog wore her statement piece with jeans and a T-shirt.

"*Any of the new dog treats I have. Boney Jack picked Bear for one of his secret good deeds this year! He left dog treats outside our apartment door this morning. They're in here.*" Millie patted her small pink purse. "*But Bear's not going to get any. Not a single one!*"

Millie flounced over to her friend Flora.

Charlie looked over at Wendell, who was sitting alone eating his sandwich. At least Wendell was still doing his secret good deeds. Wendell had taken the missing Boney Hand hard. Charlie was sure Wendell blamed him, because now Wendell refused even to look at Charlie.

Rupert and Jasper were playing Frisbee. Jasper threw the Frisbee too high. It sailed over Rupert's head and landed next to Charlie.

As Rupert ran over, Frog turned her back on him. Charlie picked up the Frisbee and handed it back.

"*Thanks,*" signed Rupert, suddenly, seemingly nice. It always confused Charlie when Rupert was nice. Charlie *wanted* Rupert to be nice. Rupert signed something else, something that Charlie didn't understand. Oliver interpreted.

"He asked if you heard the rumor. Willoughby is saying if it was a student who stole the Boney Hand, they can return it to the church by Friday with no questions asked."

Rupert signed something else. Then he laughed and went back to playing Frisbee.

"What did he say?" asked Charlie.

"He said, 'Now's the chance for you and Frog to return the Boney Hand without getting in trouble.' Jerk," added Oliver.

Frog tapped Charlie. "*Is he gone?*" signed Frog without turning around.

Charlie reached over so Frog would see his hand.

"*Yes,*" he signed. Then he took out his notebook and pen.

Do you know what Willoughby has been saying? he wrote.

I've seen the rumor, wrote Frog. *But I'm suspicious. Why would Willoughby say no questions would be asked if he wants to catch the thief so badly? Besides, did he forget about the death curse? There is no way a student would touch the Boney Hand!*

Once again, Charlie thought about how he seemed to have not taken the curse seriously before the hand went missing. Was Frog remembering that, too?

Oliver leaned over to see what Frog was writing.

"That," signed Oliver, agreeing. *"Not even in Grandpa's time would a CSD student dare to touch it."* He signed and then spoke for Charlie before collecting his lunch trash and leaving.

Ruthella looked up from her book.

She held out her hand for the notebook and pen.

In mystery books, wrote Ruthella, *the guilty one is usually the person everyone has overlooked.*

With a satisfied nod, Ruthella returned to her reading.

Charlie and Frog considered this new perspective.

Charlie could see Frog was thinking even if she wasn't pacing. Finally, she pointed to Ruthella, who was so lost in her book she hadn't noticed the jam dripping out of her sandwich and onto her lap.

"She's right," signed Frog, making the ASL number one with both hands. She placed one fist on top of the other, with the pinky of the top fist touching the thumb of the bottom fist. *There's someone I have overlooked,* wrote Frog, *because I did not want that person to be guilty.*

Frog was looking at Charlie with a Frog look that he had never seen before.

It was a *kind* look.

Which scared Charlie because Frog did not give kind looks. It was a look that said, "I'm really, really sorry—but you aren't going to like what I have to say next."

Charlie braced himself.

This was it. Frog was going to say Charlie was the thief. He was sure of it.

Remember, wrote Frog, *when I said that detectives must be impartial at all times? That we have to look at facts?*

Frog was all about facts. It wouldn't matter that Charlie was her friend if the facts pointed her in his direction.

Well, this suspect, continued Frog, *is going to be hard for you to take.*

"*Who?*" signed Charlie. He just wanted to get this over.

Frog ignored him. *This person,* wrote Frog, *was nearby when the Boney Hand first disappeared, as was everyone else, of course. But this person was also nearby when the Boney Hand reappeared. And this person has a motive.*

Charlie was there when the Boney Hand first disappeared.

He was there again when the Boney Hand reappeared.

As for motive? Maybe Charlie had stolen it just to

accept Rupert's dare—to show he wasn't scared. Were there any good reasons for taking a bony hand?

"Just say it," signed Charlie.

Frog took a deep breath.

"My mom."

Charlie didn't register what Frog had said for a few seconds, even though he knew the sign for "*mom.*"

Then it hit him.

No. Way.

No way would Mrs. Castle ever do that.

"Impossible," signed Charlie.

I told you it would be hard for you, wrote Frog.

Fact: We saw Mom near Blythe and Bone just before Miss Tweedy was frightened by the Boney Hand. Fact: Mom is always worried about money for our school. Final fact: Mom said that the Flying Hands Café is now super busy (aka making a ton of money) because of the disappearance of the Boney Hand.

Charlie snatched the pen from Frog. *That doesn't mean*, he wrote, *that your mom stole the Boney Hand! Or scared Miss Tweedy with it!*

"I know," signed Frog. She calmly reached for the pen. *But it does mean that Mom has a motive*, she wrote. *We haven't been able to find a motive until now. And I would not be doing my job if I didn't investigate her.*

"What about the curse?" signed Charlie.

Mom would risk her life for this school, wrote Frog. *She would do anything to keep our school strong. And maybe she found a way to get around the curse. My mom is very smart.*

Actually, continued Frog, *it's kind of brilliant. By taking the Boney Hand, Mom has everyone talking about our school. Everyone is coming to eat at the café! And stealing the Boney Hand is not really stealing as it belongs to the castle anyway.*

Charlie buried his head in his hands. Frog patted him on the back.

How could Frog suspect her own mother? But then Charlie recalled the morning of the Fall Extravaganza. The man with the paint-splattered clothes had been there.

Charlie lifted his head.

Remember when we saw your mom in the village? wrote Charlie. *When she was with that man?*

The one with paint all over his clothes, wrote Frog.

Well, wrote Charlie, *he was also at the castle the morning of the Fall Extravaganza.*

"*What? Why didn't you tell me before?*" signed Frog.

"*Because,*" signed Charlie, "*I didn't think it was related to the Boney Hand!*"

Charlie fingerspelled RELATED. Frog showed him how to sign it. Then she signed, "*What else haven't you told me?*"

Charlie hesitated, but maybe it was important.

"*When your mom saw him that morning*," he signed, "*she looked kind of worried.*"

Charlie knew Frog was thinking the same thing. Was the man involved with the missing Boney Hand? Had he forced Mrs. Castle to be involved? Frog would say there was only one way to know for sure.

They had to investigate.

22. Horse

When lunch was over, Charlie headed to history class. Miss Davenport was interpreting for Charlie, but what she was saying never entered Charlie's brain, for it was already filled with thoughts of Mrs. Castle and the Boney Hand.

Frog had told Charlie to meet her at three o'clock at the Alice and Francine statue. Then they would search Mrs. Castle's study. Charlie couldn't—he wouldn't—believe that Mrs. Castle was guilty. He would do the opposite of Frog. While Frog was looking for proof of her mother's guilt, Charlie would search for proof of her innocence.

After history class, Charlie headed to the barn. He hadn't been to the barn since the Boney Hand was stolen. He couldn't bear it if Obie thought he had something to do with it.

But he missed the barn. And he missed talking with Obie.

The barn was peaceful. Even the chickens were clucking quietly. Obie signed with Darius at the far end of the stables. Max was right next to Obie. When Charlie walked in, Max nudged his body against Obie's leg and thumped his tail to let Obie know a friend was near. Max trotted over to Charlie, the top part of his ears flopping up and down. Charlie rubbed Max's head along with his soft, silky ears.

Then he went over to Reggie, a police horse that finally retired to eat hay and give rides to students. "*Horse*" was a sign Millie had taught him: You made the ASL number three, but kept your index and middle fingers together. You put your thumb on the side of your forehead and flapped the two straight fingers up and down. *Horse*.

As Charlie petted Reggie's neck, Reggie nuzzled Charlie's arm. Reggie was the cuddliest horse Charlie had ever met. Animals didn't need words. They used a different kind of language. Charlie never had trouble being understood by animals or understanding them. He wished people were that simple.

Obie came over with Max and Darius. Usually, Obie signed first. But this time he was waiting for Charlie, as if he knew Charlie had something he had to say.

And Charlie did.

He wanted to blurt out, I'm worried about the Boney Hand. It could be real, which is scary. But I'm also worried because some people think that I stole it. Even Mrs. Castle might think that I stole it! I'm worried that *you* might think I stole it. But now Frog thinks maybe it was Mrs. Castle who took it. I don't know which of those are worse. I just want everything to be back to what it was before the Fall Extravaganza!

But that just seemed like a big messy jumble of thoughts.

So Charlie asked a question instead. A question he had been thinking about for a while now. Charlie knew Obie never minded questions. He always replied, *"That's an interesting question."*

"Obie, how do you know what people are like if you never see them?" Charlie asked in Obie's hands.

"That's an interesting question," signed Obie. He thought for a moment. Then he answered Charlie's question with one of his own.

"Do you know why," asked Obie, *"I don't mind people asking me questions?"*

Charlie placed his hand under Obie's. *"No."*

"Because," Obie told him as Darius interpreted, *"I*

ask so many questions myself. I see who people are by asking questions. I ask them to tell me about themselves. I ask them to tell me about other people. I learn pieces of everyone from everyone else, and then I puzzle all those pieces together."

"*That seems like a lot of work,*" signed Charlie.

"*It is,*" agreed Obie. "*But people are many things. They're complicated. When you understand the different pieces of a person, you can really see who that person is.*"

This did not make Charlie feel better about Mrs. Castle. What if stealing the Boney Hand was one of her pieces? Mrs. Castle was good, but could she still do a bad thing?

"*Now,*" signed Obie, "*I answered your question. It's time for you to answer mine. What's wrong?*"

23. Search

At three o'clock the castle was streaming with students heading to sports practice, club meetings, internships, or jobs. Normally Charlie would be heading to track practice, but not today. He wasn't super fast, but no one on the Castle School for the Deaf track team seemed to care. Not like the school Charlie had attended when his parents were away helping northern hairy-nosed wombats. The coach at that school had said track team was only for fast people.

Charlie had surprised himself by saying to that coach, "But if I join the track team, maybe I'll learn to run faster."

"The point of track team," said the coach, "is not to learn to run faster. The point is to already run fast and win."

Charlie was not on the track team that year.

But Coach Crawford at CSD didn't care.

"Try your best," he had told Charlie. *"Have fun."*

Charlie did have fun, and the more he practiced, the faster he ran.

Charlie and Frog made their way upstairs through a narrow winding staircase. The hall with Grandpa Sol's study and Mrs. Castle's study was quiet, just like Frog had said it would be. Grandpa Sol was usually outside this time of day. Mrs. Castle was always rushing here or there. Which is why Charlie was so nervous. You never knew when and where she would pop up.

Her study door was unlocked. They quickly went inside and shut the door.

Mrs. Castle's study was bright and colorful.

And messy.

It reminded Charlie of Frog's room, except there weren't any frogs in Mrs. Castle's study. But there were books and papers and drawings on the walls that students had made for her. A dark-purple couch with lots of pillows sat in front of the tall windows. The Hudson River glittered in the afternoon sunshine as a tugboat chugged north up the river.

"Okay," signed Frog. *"Search for the Boney Hand."*

Frog signed *"search,"* the sign that Charlie's name sign was based on, by forming the letter *C,* and making circles in front of her face in the direction her palm pointed.

She pulled open a desk drawer. Using a ruler, Frog carefully poked around inside without disturbing the contents. She wasn't going to take any chances with accidentally touching the Boney Hand.

Charlie did not want to reach into a drawer, ruler or no ruler. It felt wrong—a violation of Mrs. Castle's trust.

He would use only his eyes.

He kept telling himself that he had to do this to clear Mrs. Castle's name. To prove to Frog that her mother was innocent.

Frog banged on the desk. Charlie turned around.

"What are you doing?" signed Frog.

"I'm looking!" signed Charlie.

"What about your hands? You have to use your hands!"

Charlie shook his head.

"Use a ruler! Then you won't touch it!"

Charlie shook his head again.

"Fine! Just use your eyes! And your ears! Let me know if you hear someone coming."

That Charlie could do.

While Frog rifled through her mother's things with the determination of a detective, Charlie inspected the bookshelves. Books were everywhere in the castle. And there wasn't space on these shelves to hide a bony hand because they were so tightly packed with books.

Frog said you could learn a lot about a person by the type of books she read. Mrs. Castle was like Ruthella—she read everything. There were cookbooks and science books, mystery books and history books. There were books with big words that Chief Paley would love, and books with easy words that would be perfect for Millie.

Between the bookshelves and the tall windows was a space. Charlie peered in. No hand.

Just then, he heard footsteps in the hallway.

Someone was coming.

• • •

Charlie stomped on the wooden floor.

Frog spun around.

He pointed to his ear and then to the door. Frog dove behind the purple couch. Charlie followed, tumbling to the floor.

Behind the couch, a large painting leaned up against the wall. The entire canvas was covered in shades of red.

Blood red.

And in the blood-red center hovered a hideous bony hand.

24. Nothing

The study door opened.

Charlie could hear the soft sounds of sign language. It sounded like two people. Charlie held up two fingers. Frog nodded as he listened.

The rubbing of wood as a desk drawer opened.

The crackle of shuffling papers.

The smacking of hands as they formed a sign.

"Please don't let it be Mrs. Castle," Charlie silently chanted. "Please don't let it be Mrs. Castle."

Another drawer was opened.

And then . . . silence.

Charlie held his breath.

Footsteps approached.

A face loomed over them.

Oliver. It was only Oliver.

Charlie breathed.

But he stopped breathing again when Mrs. Castle also appeared.

"Stand up!" signed Mrs. Castle. *"Right now!"*

Shamefaced, Charlie stepped around the couch, as did Frog.

Oliver did not need to interpret Mrs. Castle's question.

"What are you two doing in my study?"

What were they doing? They were looking for evidence that Mrs. Castle stole the Boney Hand. But Charlie couldn't say that.

"Nothing," signed Charlie, making the letter *O* with both of his hands and shaking them sideways slightly. Frog had her arms crossed, looking like Dorrie McCann on the front cover of her first mystery.

"Frog?" Mrs. Castle gave her daughter her own steely-eyed look. Frog took a deep breath.

"Did you take the Boney Hand," signed Frog, *"so the Flying Hands Café would get more customers?"*

Charlie could not believe Frog had just accused her own mother of stealing.

Neither could Oliver. "Whoa," said Oliver.

And neither could Mrs. Castle.

"*What?*" she signed. "*You think I stole the Boney Hand?*" Mrs. Castle's finger stabbed her chest. "*Me?*"

Frog marched behind the couch and pulled out the painting of the Boney Hand.

Frog's hands flew. Oliver saw Charlie struggling to understand, so he interpreted.

"*You had a motive,*" signed Frog as Oliver spoke. "*You said business is now booming at the café. And we saw you in the village with that man the night Miss Tweedy saw the Boney Hand. Who is he? Why were you with him?*"

When her mother didn't answer, Frog stamped her foot. Her pearl necklace quivered.

"*I'm a detective!*" signed Frog. "*Even if you are my mother and I love you this much*"—Frog stretched her arms as wide as she could—"*I have to uncover the truth!*"

Frog dropped her hands to her sides, as if they were tired from what they had just signed. Mrs. Castle stared at the painting and then at Frog.

Charlie and Oliver each took a step backward, preparing for the explosion. But it never came.

Instead, Mrs. Castle regarded Frog with a gleam of—was it respect? Respect for Frog as a detective and doing what she had to do? The look lasted just for a second, and then Mrs. Castle was back.

"*You don't go into people's private spaces,*" she signed, "*without asking permission first!*"

"*A detective can't ask permission,*" Frog pointed out. "*A detective has to detect!*"

Mrs. Castle pressed her lips together. "*I don't have time to discuss this right now,*" she signed. "*We'll talk about it tonight.*"

"*Charlie and I have tickets for the movie tonight,*" signed Frog.

Charlie was sure Mrs. Castle would say they couldn't go, but instead she just nodded.

"*Tomorrow morning, then,*" signed Mrs. Castle. "*Now please leave.*"

Frog started to protest but then thought better of it. Charlie and Frog left Mrs. Castle's study and walked down the narrow winding staircase. Once they arrived at the great hall with the Alice and Francine statue, Frog wrote: *Did you see what happened? Mom didn't deny stealing the hand!*

That was awful, wrote Charlie. *I can't believe you accused your mom!*

You were there searching with me! wrote Frog. *Why did she have that weird painting of the Boney Hand?*

Charlie was about to write, *I will never believe your mom stole it,* when he heard a scream.

It was Millie.

• • •

They dashed up the wide stone staircase and found Millie huddled outside the Castle family apartment.

"Millie! What happened?" signed Frog.

Then Mrs. Castle and Oliver were there.

Mrs. Castle scooped up Millie, who clung to her mother and buried her head in the crook of her neck.

Finally, Millie lifted her head and signed, with Oliver interpreting for Charlie.

"I was just about to go inside our house," signed Millie, *"and then I saw something there."* Millie pointed down the hall, past the wide staircase. *"It was the Boney Hand,"* she sobbed, *"pointing a finger at me!"* Millie buried her head again.

Mrs. Castle tapped her on her back. Millie lifted her head. *"Where is Bear?"* asked her mother.

"With Boris!" signed Millie. *"Bear went with him because Bear loves him! What if Bear loves him more than me?"* This brought fresh tears to Millie's eyes.

Frog hurried to the end of the hall. Charlie and Oliver followed. The three of them paused and braced themselves before turning the corner.

Nothing was there.

25. Popcorn

Late that afternoon, Charlie watched Cornelius van Dyke peacefully read a thick history book at the Castle-on-the-Hudson Museum (and Historical Society).

Charlie, on the other hand, felt anything but peaceful. He sat cross-legged on his chair and gazed at the floor, wondering where the Boney Hand would next appear.

Frog did nothing to calm Charlie's fear. Instead, she confirmed it.

You should be afraid, wrote Frog. *The Boney Hand has been seen OUTSIDE the castle and OUTSIDE in the village. Today it was seen INSIDE the castle. The next place we might see it is somewhere INSIDE in the village.*

Charlie did not like Frog's reasoning. He didn't like it at all. He gazed around the floor one more time.

If the Boney Hand really is alive, wrote Frog, *all we can do is try to keep safe and catch it if we can. But we don't know FOR SURE if it's alive—which means we also have to assume SOMEONE stole the Boney Hand. Someone scared Miss Tweedy with it. And now that someone scared Millie.*

Frog paused for a moment and then signed, *"At least we know it's not my mom. No way would Mom scare Millie like that. But who would? And why?"*

They tried to focus on their homework, but it wasn't easy. Charlie thought back to what had happened with Millie. Rupert and some other kids had also come to the top of the stairs and saw Millie crying about the Boney Hand—and Charlie and Frog had been right there.

"See what I mean?" signed Rupert.

Charlie knew Rupert's hands would soon be spinning a story about what happened, ensnaring the other kids in his web.

If someone did steal it, I just wish they'd return it, wrote Charlie. *Mr. Willoughby said he wouldn't ask any more questions. Then everything can be back to normal.*

I don't trust Willoughby, wrote Frog. *He has an ulterior motive.*

What does "ulterior" mean? asked Charlie.

It means, wrote Frog, *there's a nefarious reason why Willoughby said the thief has until Friday to return the*

Boney Hand, no questions asked. I just don't know what it is yet. And Rupert is telling everyone we're pretending to search for the hand when really we are the ones who took it. I hate Rupert.

"*You shouldn't hate anyone,*" signed Charlie.

Frog ignored him. *Are you one hundred percent sure,* she wrote, *that you heard Rupert laughing outside the graveyard the night the hand was stolen?*

"*I'm sure,*" signed Charlie. And he was. Pretty sure.

After another half hour of pretending to do homework, Frog pointed to the clock and signed, "*Time to grab dinner and then head to the movie!*"

She began putting her schoolbooks into her backpack.

"*Do we have to go?*" signed Charlie.

It's tradition! wrote Frog. *Everyone goes, except for the little kids of course. And maybe when we're watching, we'll know what to do next. You never know where our next clue could come from!*

Frog waved to Cornelius, who barely looked up from his book to grunt good-bye.

Charlie walked outside behind Frog.

He really didn't want to go.

Not to *this* movie.

Not now. Not ever.

• • •

The village of Castle-on-the-Hudson had one movie theater. During the year, it showed all sorts of films, but for one week it played one movie only: *The Boney Hand*.

The movie theater was sold out, because visitors who came to the village for its coffee shops, quaint stores, and the fall beauty of the Hudson Valley were also riveted by the idea that a bony hand might be wandering around.

Charlie and Frog stood in line for popcorn and lemonade, even though they just had bagel sandwiches at Finkelstein's. Charlie practiced the sign for *"popcorn"* by facing his two fists toward his body. He raised one fist and flicked his index finger up. Then he lowered that fist and index finger and raised the other fist and popped that index finger up. Doing this several times made the sign for *"popcorn,"* which to Charlie looked like popcorn popping.

When they found their seats, Frog handed him her popcorn.

"I'm going to the bathroom," she signed. *"Do you have to go?"*

Charlie shook his head and took a sip of his lemonade.

"You should go anyway before the movie starts," signed Frog as she left.

Oliver was here with his friends in the back of the theater. Ruthella sat near the front, reading. Wendell was next to her, eagerly waiting for the movie about his hero,

Boney Jack, to begin. Rupert and Jasper sat two rows in front of Charlie. Rupert was signing to Jasper. Jasper looked hurt and shook his head no. Rupert nodded yes and laughed.

Charlie hated that laugh.

Hating a laugh was different from hating a person, he told himself.

Boris, who was not interpreting tonight, was in the theater with his own bucket of popcorn. He leaned over and tapped Charlie on the shoulder.

"How you doing, Charlie?" asked Boris.

"Not great," said Charlie. "How about you?"

"I love it here," said Boris as he munched his popcorn. "Wait." Boris stopped eating. "Why aren't you great?"

"Because," said Charlie, "everyone thinks Frog and I had something to do with the missing Boney Hand. Or maybe worse, the Boney Hand crawled away on its own."

"Bummer," said Boris. But he didn't seem too bummed as he ate another handful of popcorn. And he didn't deny anything Charlie said. "You and Frog are a good team," Boris remarked.

"What do you mean?" asked Charlie.

"Frog is the lead detective, right? And you're her right-hand man."

Charlie nodded. "I like helping Frog. I don't want to be a detective, though. I don't know what I want to be when I grow up." For some reason it bothered Charlie that he didn't know yet. After all, Frog knew. Oliver knew. Boris knew.

"The important thing is you have each other's backs," Boris continued. "You take care of each other. If anyone is going to figure out what's going on, it's you two." Boris dug into his popcorn again.

"I hope so," said Charlie.

Frog slid back into her seat as two ushers came to the front of the theater. The lights flashed on and off to get everyone's attention. One usher signed, and the other usher spoke.

"*Welcome!*" the ushers greeted the audience. "*The movie you're about to watch was made thirty years ago by a film class at Castle School for the Deaf. The Boney Hand, as you all know, is currently missing. But don't be afraid—we did a careful sweep of the theater. We are ALMOST positive there's no bony hand crawling around in here!*"

The audience laughed and shifted nervously in their seats.

"*No need to turn off your cell phones as they don't work here anyway,*" the ushers continued. "*The movie is captioned for the signing-impaired. And now we present the classic film*—The Boney Hand!"

The house lights dimmed.

The movie opened with two children playing on the bank of the Hudson River. A ship sailed around the bend—a pirate ship! Charlie was impressed with the students' movie-making skills. The ship looked real, and they had actually filmed it on the river.

"Pirates!" the children signed, and ran into a house.

A woman was making bread. When the children told her pirates were coming, she clutched her chest, her eyes full of fear. Outside, the pirate ship sailed closer and closer. The pirates heaved themselves into a small wooden boat, rowed to the shore, and swarmed into the house.

"Where's your silver and gold?" the pirates signed as they entered the house.

"Give us that puppy!" one pirate demanded.

"Give us your cow!" another pirate ordered.

But one pirate stood to the side and never stole. When the plundering and pillaging was over, Boney Jack waited for the pirates to fall asleep. Boney Jack picked up the puppy and returned it in the dark of night. He led the cow home in the wee hours of the morning. He collected as much stolen silver and gold as he dared and brought it back to the grateful villagers.

Charlie recognized a much younger Grandpa Sol as one of the farmers. And he recognized many of the hearing villagers who were extras in the film. A very young Miss Tweedy, who had pointy glasses even back then, had trouble not looking at the camera.

Then Boney Jack was accused of thievery. No one

defended him. No one spoke up. A trial ensued. And Boney Jack was found guilty.

Boney Jack signed his last words as the villagers watched.

"I tried to do good," said Boney Jack. And he said no more. A pirate tied his hands.

Boney Jack walked the plank and sank under the waves.

It was then Charlie realized he had finished his lemonade and desperately had to go to the bathroom. Why hadn't he listened to Frog? He would go fast so he wouldn't miss much.

"Bathroom," he signed to Frog and stood up.

"Told you!" signed Frog, satisfied she was right. She moved her legs sideways so Charlie could get out.

The woman selling popcorn was gone. The lobby was empty and quiet.

Too quiet.

Boney Hand quiet.

Charlie would have gone right back into the theater if he didn't have to go so badly. It would be fine, he told himself. He looked around for the bathroom. He saw a sign pointing down the stairs.

"It's fine. Everything is fine," Charlie chanted out loud.

He dodged several large cobwebs as he walked

downstairs into a musty-smelling hallway. He found the small bathroom at the end of the long hall. Charlie quickly went in and locked the door.

He made it.

The bathroom was brightly lit and decorated with old movie posters.

Boris had told Charlie the movies they showed in the village theater were all excellent, and Charlie should watch as many—

Tap-tap, pound.

Someone knocked on the bathroom door.

Tap-pound-pound, tap-pound, tap-tap-tap.

Well, they would just have to wait until Charlie was—

Pound-pound, tap.

—finished.

His chest tightened. Charlie knew that knocking.

Tap-tap, pound . . . tap-pound-pound, tap-pound, tap-tap-tap . . . pound-pound, tap.

It was the same pattern of knocking Charlie had heard in the hallway of the castle.

Tap-tap, pound . . . tap-pound-pound, tap-pound, tap-tap-tap . . . pound-pound, tap.

Who . . . or what . . . was doing it?

Tap-tap, pound . . . tap-pound-pound, tap-pound, tap-tap-tap . . . pound-pound, tap.

Charlie was all alone down here.

Tap-tap, pound . . . tap-pound-pound, tap-pound, tap-tap-tap . . . pound-pound, tap.

He finished going to the bathroom, his heart thudding hard and heavy.

Tap-tap, pound . . . tap-pound-pound, tap-pound, tap-tap-tap . . . pound-pound, tap.

With trembling hands, Charlie turned on the faucet.

He couldn't open the door yet because he had to wash his hands.

He had to wash his hands really well.

After all, the Centers for Disease Control and Prevention did say that washing hands was the most important thing you could do to avoid spreading germs.

Tap-tap, pound . . . tap-pound-pound, tap-pound, tap-tap-tap . . . pound-pound, tap.

Charlie kept washing his hands.

Tap-tap, pound . . .

And washing.

Tap-pound-pound, tap-pound, tap-tap-tap . . .

And washing.

Pound-pound, tap.

Finally he turned off the water. He had to open the door. He had no choice. He had to leave.

Charlie wished he had taken martial arts, like Frog had, instead of joining track. Running fast didn't help you if you were trapped. What should he do?

What. Should. He. Do?

Whatshouldhedo? Whatshouldhedo? Whatshouldhedo?

Charlie pulled back the latch and flung open the door.

The hallway was empty.

• • •

Charlie fell into his seat just as the caretaker keeled over on the big screen. When the teacher found him on the floor, the caretaker told her what the Boney Hand had fingerspelled:

NO . . . ONE . . . SAW . . .

The caretaker gave one final gasp and died.

Other people arrived at the church. The teacher took off her coat and carefully picked up the Boney Hand. She placed the hand, with the coat still around it, inside a wooden box.

The caretaker was buried in the graveyard.

The last frame of the movie was a group of students standing on a bluff, looking out over the Hudson as the sun set, the river ablaze with orange and red.

Words scrolled on the screen.

The Boney Hand was eventually placed inside a glass dome, where it resides today at Castle School for the Deaf. Once a year the hand is on display for everyone to see.

The Boney Hand has not moved again—yet.

The credits ended and the house lights came up.

Charlie fumbled with his pen and notebook in his rush to tell Frog.

I heard knocking on the bathroom door! wrote Charlie. *It was the same pattern of knocking I heard in the castle!*

What pattern? wrote Frog.

I heard this knocking pattern the other day, when I was walking to Grandpa Sol's study, Charlie explained. *Someone or something just knocked that same way again!*

Why didn't you tell me this before? demanded Frog.

Before Charlie could answer, she grabbed his arm.

"Did you see that?" she signed.

"See what?" asked Charlie.

"Rupert," Frog whisper-signed. She pointed to the exit door. She would tell Charlie outside.

But outside the theater, Chief Paley was waiting for Charlie.

"It's your grandparents," said the chief.

26. Help

"We've been waiting for you, Charlie!" said Grandma Tickler when Charlie and Chief Paley walked into the kitchen.

"Ayuh," said Grandpa Tickler.

Charlie's grandparents were seated at the table with a deck of cards spread out. Thankfully, they had taken off their detective outfits and were dressed in normal clothes. Yvette was washing dishes at the kitchen sink.

"You can play, too, Chief Paley," said Grandma.

"I'm here on police business," said the chief. "It's about Walter Simple."

"Grandma and Grandpa," said Charlie, "what did you do to Mr. Simple?"

"We did our job, Charlie," said Grandma. "We suspected Walter Simple of stealing the Boney Hand, so we did what you're supposed to do with a suspect!"

Charlie was afraid to ask, but he did so anyway. "And what is that?"

"We pinned him to the wall!" said Grandma.

"I wish that were a figure of speech," said Yvette over her shoulder. "But it's not."

Charlie remembered what Grandma Tickler had said yesterday when she talked about catching a suspect. She mentioned pinning a guilty person to the wall.

"It was just a nudge with the taxi," said Grandma. "Herman is very careful, and Walter Simple is strong as an ox."

"That's factual," said Chief Paley. "Even though he was sandwiched between the taxi and a lamppost, he's fine."

"We couldn't get Walter to confess," said Grandma. "We're going to need another method. And," she added, "Herman wants us to pay for the damage to the taxi."

"Ayuh," said Grandpa.

Charlie turned to Chief Paley. "They mentioned something about pinning people yesterday," said Charlie, "but I didn't think they would actually do it."

"Never underestimate octogenarians," said Chief Paley.

"Now that's the truth," said Yvette without turning around from the sink.

"Underestimating octogenarians is a common pitfall in law enforcement," said the chief. "As we were always reminded during my academy training—senior citizens are more than capable of nefarious acts, as well as courageous ones."

"You bet we are," said Grandma.

"Ayuh," Grandpa chimed in.

"Grandma and Grandpa, you promised to wait for me before you did any more investigating. Remember?" said Charlie.

"We had our fingers crossed," said Grandma Tickler. "Promises don't count when you cross your fingers!"

"It's fortuitous Walter Simple is declining to press charges," said Chief Paley.

"When crime is a fact, good people act!" said Grandma. "Good people do good things!"

Grandma Tickler pointed to the certificate that Vince Vinelli had sent along with their Vince Vinelli When Crime Is a Fact, Good People Act detective kit. It hung in a frame above the kitchen sink.

"How was pinning Walter Simple with a taxicab a good thing?" asked Yvette as she reached for the dishtowel.

"Because, Yvette, we were helping. Frog taught us that sign."

Grandma Tickler made a thumbs-up with one hand. She put her other hand, palm up, underneath it and lifted her hands upward. "*Help.*"

"Ayuh," said Grandpa.

He reached out and squeezed Charlie's hand.

"Help," said Grandpa. "Helping our Charlie."

It was so rare to hear Grandpa Tickler say anything but "ayuh" that everyone, especially Charlie, let those words float in the air for a moment.

"Our Charlie."

"Helping our Charlie."

Chief Paley cleared her throat. "Irma and Irving, I will drop this matter with the stipulation you will not do anything like this again."

"Promise!" said Grandma.

"For real?" said Yvette.

"No fingers crossed, Yvette," said Grandma. "But, Chief Paley, now that you're here, we need some professional guidance, don't we, Irving?"

"Ayuh."

"You see," explained Grandma, "besides the Boney Hand case, Irving and I have been trying to solve the Mystery of the Missing TV Remote Control. But then, at lunch, a new case presented itself to us. Didn't it, Irving?"

"Ayuh."

Chief Paley flipped open her notepad. "What's the situation?"

Grandma Tickler went over to the refrigerator. She opened the freezer door, reached inside, and pulled out Grandpa Tickler's plaid boxer shorts—frozen stiff.

"It's the Mystery of the Frozen Underwear!" said Grandma.

Charlie looked away. It didn't seem right to be staring at Grandpa Tickler's underwear, even if it was frozen.

Especially if it was frozen.

"We've already interrogated Yvette," said Grandma. "And Yvette said—Yvette, what did you say again?"

"I said, 'Why on earth would I want to freeze Irving's boxer shorts?'" said Yvette.

"That's exactly what she told us," said Grandma. "Chief Paley, we need your help!"

• • •

Just before bedtime, the phone rang. His grandparents were already upstairs, so Charlie picked up the black phone receiver.

"Tickler residence. Charlie speaking."

"It's me, your mother!" said Mrs. Tickler.

"And me, your father!" said Mr. Tickler.

"Hi, Mom and Dad," he said.

"Charlie, we had a phone conversation with Mrs. Castle today," said his father.

"You did?" said Charlie. "How?"

"Mrs. Castle called us using an interpreter," said his mother. "She told us that the Boney Hand situation has been stressful for you and that she's concerned about you. I told her we were concerned as well! In fact, I told her we had used that exact word the last time we talked with you!"

"But we think the interpreter misunderstood," said Mr. Tickler. "Because he told us Mrs. Castle said, 'Animals don't need your help. Charlie needs your help.'"

Charlie couldn't believe Mrs. Castle would say that to his parents.

"Mrs. Castle told us the interpreter did not make a mistake," said Mrs. Tickler.

"It made no sense," said Mr. Tickler. "I told her Charlie has a protected safe place to live. He doesn't have to worry about his home."

"Or worry about his food!" said Mrs. Tickler.

"Or fear getting eaten by a predator!"

"Alistair, perhaps the answer to what Mrs. Castle meant is in one of our new books."

"Good thinking, Myra! Let's take a look."

His parents' voices became muffled. It sounded as if they had put the phone down on their hotel bed. They had forgotten Charlie was there. He gently hung up the phone and went upstairs to the bedroom his parents used when they weren't helping animals. Charlie looked at some of the parenting books they had borrowed from the library:

Children Are Not Pets

Become the Parent You Wish You Had

If Parenting Was Easy, Anyone Could Do It!

If parents could find answers in these books about their kids, maybe kids could find answers about their parents. Because his parents, Charlie realized, were the real mystery. Charlie picked up *Children Are Not Pets* and went to brush his teeth.

27. Mean

It was the first blustery day of autumn. Falling leaves spiraled and spun over the streets of the village. Charlie bent his head into the wind and tucked his hands into his coat as he walked to the gondola.

He watched Mr. Simple crank gears and pull levers as the gondola rode the cable from the castle. He hoped the wind wouldn't get any stronger. The gondola wasn't supposed to operate when it got too windy, but Charlie had to get to the castle to talk to Frog about last night. Not only about the knocking on the bathroom door, but also what Frog had seen Rupert do after the movie was over.

When the gondola reached the village, Mr. Simple stopped cranking and flashed his signal light. Charlie stood between two tourists clutching their laptops and cell phones, most likely heading to breakfast at the Flying Hands Café.

Charlie had hoped Mr. Simple would forget what his grandparents had done to him yesterday.

Mr. Simple hadn't forgotten. He glowered at Charlie.

"I'm really sorry," Charlie began as he handed him a dollar for the gondola ride.

"Your ... your ... your ..." Mr. Simple spluttered. Steam seemed to spurt out of his ears, just like in the cartoons. "Grandparents!" Mr. Simple finally spit out the word.

"I know," said Charlie. "I feel the same way."

"They ... they ... they ..." Mr. Simple spluttered some more.

"They think you stole the Boney Hand." Charlie helped Mr. Simple say it. "But don't worry," said Charlie. "Frog and I don't think you did it."

Mr. Simple slammed the gondola door shut.

The gondola jerked forward with a vengeance.

• • •

Frog was working in the Flying Hands Café before school started, serving waffles, pancakes, and eggs.

There were two prices at the Flying Hands Café.

Pancakes, for instance, were $4.99 if you used your hands to order them, whether it was signing or finger-spelling or gesturing or pointing. Pancakes were $9.99 if you used only your voice to order.

Charlie watched two hearing customers hesitate to walk between two signing Deaf customers. They couldn't walk around them because of how the tables were set up. Finally, the hearing people ducked their heads and rushed between them. Charlie had learned the right way to walk between two people signing: Just walk between them normally. The signers will sign around you.

Frog saw Charlie. She finished serving her table and pulled him over.

"What happened with your grandparents last night?" signed Frog. She wore long sparkly earrings that shimmied as she signed.

"You don't want to know," signed Charlie.

Frog considered this. *"Knowing your grandparents, you're probably right,"* she agreed.

"That," signed Charlie. That was exactly it. *"What did your mom say to you about finding us in her study?"*

Frog glanced at her mother, who was talking with customers. She pulled out her pen and notebook from her apron pocket. Frog didn't want anyone to see what she was signing.

Mom's been so busy with the café, wrote Frog, *that she hasn't talked to me yet! That's good, because last night I saw Rupert sign something to Jasper right after the movie was over.*

Charlie knew Frog liked to make Charlie ask, so he did.

"What?" asked Charlie.

Rupert signed, "We have it—ha-ha," wrote Frog.

She looked at Charlie, waiting for him to understand.

You think he meant, "We have the Boney Hand"? wrote Charlie.

"That!" signed Frog.

But what about the curse? asked Charlie.

Remember at the end of the movie? When the teacher takes off her coat and picks up the Boney Hand with it?

You think a coat will keep you from being cursed?

You aren't touching it, Frog pointed out. *The coat is. What if Rupert thought the same thing?* Frog, like Charlie, was writing fast and messy.

But what about the fact, wrote Charlie, *that I heard Rupert laughing OUTSIDE the graveyard wall right before the hand disappeared?*

No offense, wrote Frog, *but I don't trust hearing. I trust SEEING. And you didn't SEE that it was Rupert.*

Charlie wasn't offended. At this point he wasn't sure he trusted his eyes or his ears anymore. *So you think it was Rupert who stole the hand and Rupert who's been doing the knocking?* asked Charlie.

"*Yes,*" signed Frog.

Did you see him get out of his seat when I went to the bathroom? he asked.

Frog shook her head. *I didn't,* she wrote. *But I'll ask some other students if they did.*

Charlie had one more question.

What about motive? asked Charlie. *What's Rupert's motive for stealing the Boney Hand?*

Frog's eyes narrowed.

"*His motive,*" signed Frog, "*is that he's MEAN.*"

Frog fingerspelled MEAN and then showed Charlie how to sign it. She held one open hand near her face, and the other open hand near her chest. She brought the top hand down past the bottom hand as both hands changed into the ASL letter *A*. Frog made a mean face to match the sign.

He likes to scare people, wrote Frog. *He thinks it's funny. I'm going to prove that Rupert stole the Boney Hand. I'll solve this case and prove I am a detective!*

Charlie wanted Rupert to be guilty. He especially wanted Rupert to be guilty because of what Rupert had said to Frog. But you can't just accuse someone.

We need proof, wrote Charlie.

Then we find proof, wrote Frog. *Although being a bully should be proof enough.*

Being a bully doesn't mean Rupert stole the Boney Hand,

he wrote. *If we blame him without proof, then we're the bullies.*

That's one way to look at it, wrote Frog. *Other people might call it justice.*

Charlie gave Frog one of her own are-you-kidding-me looks.

Frog sighed.

"*Okay,*" she signed. "*We find proof.*"

28. Pay Attention

All afternoon Charlie and Frog carefully watched Rupert, looking for proof of his guilt. They both had science class with him. Rupert made comments about Charlie and Frog and whomever else he wanted to pick on in that moment.

Except when the teacher was watching. Then Rupert was perfect. It amazed Charlie how good Rupert was at looking perfect. The skeleton in the corner of the science room leered at Charlie with its awful grin.

It wasn't until dinner that they saw something.

The dining hall was a long, elegant room that stretched the length of the castle. Charlie sometimes stayed for dinner, especially when it was pizza, like tonight. The pizza was delicious at Castle School for the Deaf, but neither Charlie nor Frog tasted it.

They sat at their small round table and pretended to eat as they watched Rupert.

Frog told Charlie that none of the kids she asked had seen Rupert leave the movie theater. But then again, they were all watching the movie, not Rupert.

Nothing out of the ordinary happened at first. Rupert ate numerous slices of pizza. Jasper hardly ate at all. But then Rupert and Jasper began writing notes to each other. There was only one reason to write notes when you were a fluent signer—you were saying something you didn't want the other kids to see you sign. After a flurry of notes back and forth, Rupert nodded.

"Okay," Rupert signed. *"We do it after dinner."*

Jasper didn't respond.

Rupert punched Jasper, who grimaced and rubbed his shoulder. Jasper was much bigger than Rupert. Charlie was sure he could punch much harder, too. But he didn't. He didn't even tell Rupert to stop hitting him. He said nothing.

With his elbows bent, Rupert brought his hands by either side of his face, fingers together, palms facing toward each other. He quickly moved his hands forward and backward twice.

"*Pay attention!*" signed Rupert. "*We do it after dinner,*" he repeated.

Jasper nodded.

At the next table Wendell looked scared, as if Rupert might punch him next.

Frog reached for her notebook.

Finally, wrote Frog. *We have a lead.*

Rupert and Jasper stood up, cleared their plates, and slipped out of the dining hall.

Charlie and Frog cleared their dishes and hurried outside after them. They stood at the castle doors, staring into the darkness. Where had they gone? The lights of the village twinkled across the river.

"What are you doing?" said a voice.

Charlie jumped. But it was only Oliver.

Oliver tapped Frog, who also jumped.

"*Stop it!*" signed Frog.

"*I can't,*" he signed. "*I've been ordered to watch you both.*" Oliver signed and then spoke this last part for Charlie.

"*By who?*" signed Frog.

"*By Mom,*" signed Oliver. "*She's worried about both of you. She doesn't know you're out here. But she will know unless—*"

Oliver paused as a group of kids left the castle and headed to the dorms. When they had passed, Oliver continued.

"—*unless you tell me what you're doing!*"

"*We're following someone,*" signed Frog. "*Now we've lost them.*" Frog peered once again into the darkness.

Frog pointed. "*There!*"

Charlie could barely see Jasper. It seemed he had dropped something in the grass and was looking for it. But no Rupert.

GO AWAY, Frog fingerspelled to Oliver.

"*No!*" he signed.

Jasper found whatever he had been looking for and started walking. Frog didn't have time to argue. They had to follow Jasper before he disappeared again.

• • •

Jasper stopped at the wooden door that was the entrance to the graveyard. Where was Rupert? Why hadn't he waited for Jasper? The old wooden door opened smoothly for Jasper. Even though Obie wouldn't go inside the graveyard, he had oiled the door for the people coming to the Fall Extravaganza.

Both Charlie and Oliver hesitated. It might be fine for Frog to go alone into the cemetery with a bony hand on the loose—but it wasn't fine for them. But Frog was already through the door before they could sign, "*Let's think about this for a minute.*"

Charlie and Oliver sighed and hurried after her.

Jasper wasn't heading toward the church. Instead he walked farther into the graveyard. Charlie shivered in the cold—he hadn't had time to grab his fleece coat.

In the light of the moon, Charlie saw Jasper suddenly stop and turn around.

Charlie, Frog, and Oliver crouched behind a headstone:

SILAS P. FRANKFURTER
1798–1871
HE SAW EVERYTHING, YET SAID NOTHING.

Frog peeked over the headstone. She gave a thumbs-up and gestured, *"Let's go!"*

Charlie did not have a good feeling about this, but Jasper kept walking. He paused by another headstone and knelt down.

"What's he doing?" signed Frog.

"Praying?" suggested Oliver.

They continued to walk closer. Jasper seemed to be holding something in his hands.

They walked closer.

And closer.

This did not feel right. In fact, everything inside Charlie was screaming "Run!" But Charlie didn't run. He kept walking toward the bent figure of Jasper.

He felt something tickle the back of his neck.

Charlie swatted it with his hand.

It brushed his neck again.

He turned around.

The Boney Hand hung midair—one bony finger pointing at Charlie.

. . .

Charlie screamed as he stumbled backward and fell. The Boney Hand swung through the air and landed on Frog's head. Frog screeched and batted it away before falling to the ground next to Charlie. Oliver squealed, even though the Boney Hand hadn't touched him.

The Boney Hand slowly rose into the air. Frog jumped up and snatched it. Charlie couldn't believe it— Frog was holding the Boney Hand with her bare hands!

Someone jumped out of a tree, laughing so hard he clutched his stomach.

Rupert.

Charlie saw why Frog had grabbed the Boney Hand.

It was plastic, with a piece of fishing line dangling from it.

Frog threw it to the ground in disgust. Her hands were flying as she told the boys what she thought of them.

"Inappropriate language" was how Oliver chose to interpret what Frog was saying to them.

But Frog's sign choices didn't bother Rupert. He

high-fived Jasper (who seemed reluctant to raise his hand and high-five him back) and then fell over laughing again. Charlie's chest hurt from his heart pounding. Could you have a heart attack at his age? It sure felt like it.

Rupert signed, *"You're so easy. You think you're a detective. Some detective!"* Oliver interpreted when it was clear Charlie wasn't following.

"Did you steal the Boney Hand?" Frog shouted at him in sign. *"Did you scare Miss Tweedy and Millie with it? Did you try to scare Charlie by knocking? If you're guilty, we ARE going to find out!"*

But Rupert didn't answer any of Frog's questions. For a moment, he looked confused. Then he signed, *"No one will believe you. Everyone believes you two are guilty."* Rupert's smile, the smile adults found so charming, was full of spite and satisfaction.

Looking at Rupert, Charlie suddenly thought of Obie's questions about everyone—questions Obie asked so that he would understand everyone else. Obie said you had to see all sides of a person in order to really *see* that person. Obie had asked a question about Rupert. Now Charlie asked it himself.

"Why," Charlie signed, *"are you so mean?"*

Rupert looked startled, as if he had never considered that question before. Perhaps no one had ever asked him.

But Charlie really wanted to know.

What had Charlie or Frog ever done to Rupert to make him so hateful? What had anyone done to make him so hateful?

Rupert looked unsure of himself for a moment.

It was as if another Rupert was now in front of Charlie, thinking, really thinking about what Charlie had just said. *Why am I so mean?*

Then he blinked and smiled.

Mean Rupert was back.

"Loser!" Rupert signed to Charlie and Frog.

He walked out of the graveyard with Jasper in tow. Frog threw the fake hand after them.

Charlie, Frog, and Oliver stood in the quiet cemetery, breathing hard. Rupert's words played over again in Charlie's head: Everyone believes you two are guilty. Everyone.

But it wasn't fair because it wasn't true.

It. Wasn't. True.

Instead of feeling sad or hurt, Charlie felt angry.

Frog paced in the graveyard, fuming.

"We aren't guilty," Charlie told Oliver. "We didn't do anything wrong."

"I believe you," said Oliver. "But you're going to have to find out what happened to the real Boney Hand to prove it."

To prove it to everyone else. How do you convince everyone else?

Charlie thought about the first mystery he and Frog had solved. How both he and Frog had learned to look within to find their own power. If people were going to see what they wanted to see, how did you have power over that? How did you have power over a mean person like Rupert?

Charlie didn't have any power over Rupert.

But, Charlie realized, then the opposite must also be true—Rupert didn't have any power over Charlie.

Unless, of course, Charlie gave him his power. And Charlie wouldn't do that. He would keep his power and use it for himself.

A calm feeling flooded over him.

Frog stopped pacing.

"We have to think," signed Frog as Oliver interpreted. *"We have to think hard—harder than we ever have thought before. We have to solve this case. I know the clues are right in front of us. We just aren't seeing them."*

29. Deaf

When Charlie came downstairs the next morning, he found Grandma and Grandpa Tickler standing in the living room, still in their bathrobes. They were studying the jelly-bean bowl that sat on the table between their two E-Z chair recliners.

"What happened?" asked Charlie. "What's wrong?"

"Yvette refilled the jelly-bean bowl yesterday with a brand-new bag," said Grandma. "We haven't eaten any yet. But now look!"

Charlie looked into the glass bowl. Jelly beans of all colors were inside it.

"Don't you see what's wrong?" asked Grandma Tickler.

"No," said Charlie. He rubbed his eyes and looked again. Just jelly beans.

"Yesterday there were black jelly beans," said Grandma. "Today there are none."

"Ayuh," said Grandpa Tickler.

Charlie knew when Grandma and Grandpa Tickler watched TV, they often liked to eat jelly beans. Grandma always picked out the black jelly beans and handed them to Grandpa. Charlie looked in the bowl. Grandma Tickler was right—not a single black jelly bean was in this batch.

The front door opened.

"Did you ask Yvette?" whispered Charlie.

"Yvette!" yelled Grandma. "Come in the living room, quick!"

Yvette came into the living room still wearing her hat and coat.

"Good morning, Yvette. How are you, Yvette?" said Yvette as she unbuttoned her coat. "Oh, I'm just fine, Irma. Thank you for asking."

"We have no time for niceties," said Grandma. "We have another case to solve! You, of course, are our first suspect. Yvette, did you take the black jelly beans?" She pointed to the bowl.

"Black jelly beans? Why on earth would I take the black jelly beans?" asked Yvette. "I don't even *like* black jelly beans."

"Me either," said Charlie.

"I need coffee," said Yvette. "There will be no more conversation until I have coffee." Yvette went into the kitchen.

"Charlie, we now have three mysteries we're investigating, besides yours: the Mystery of the Missing Remote Control, the Mystery of the Frozen Underwear, and the Mystery of the Stolen Jelly Beans. Irving, we have to cancel some of our doctor's appointments— we have too much detecting to do! Charlie, would you understand if the A Team can't work on the Mystery of the Disappearing Boney Hand today?"

"I would definitely understand," said Charlie.

• • •

Although Castle-on-the-Hudson was filled with old people, Charlie had never met anyone as old as Miss Lemon. Charlie, however, had never actually "met" Miss Lemon because Miss Lemon was always asleep whenever Charlie was in the school library.

Myrtle Lemon, also known by Frog as Mean Librarian or "M-L," had been the school librarian forever. Frog called her Mean Librarian because Miss Lemon did not like anyone in the library when she wasn't there, such as in the summertime. When Charlie and Frog needed to get into the school library to solve their case over the summer, Frog had to sneak the key away from her mother in order to get inside.

Miss Lemon had been the librarian when Mrs. Castle was a student, and even when Grandpa Sol was a student, too. That was why Mrs. Castle would not think of getting rid of her, even though Miss Lemon slept most of the day behind the circulation desk.

As a result, the students mostly ran the library, all the while careful not to wake Miss Lemon. Today was Ruthella's day to work. Ruthella moved slowly as she shelved books, keeping a watchful eye on Miss Lemon, who was snoring peacefully. Charlie sat at a table, studying for his science test. Frog was going to meet him here to figure out the next step in their investigation.

A book slipped out of Ruthella's hands. It landed on the floor with thump.

Miss Lemon stopped snoring and raised her head with her eyes still closed. For the longest time she stayed that way. Neither Charlie nor Ruthella moved. Finally, Miss Lemon's head floated down and nestled back into its original position. Her snoring resumed. Ruthella exhaled and continued shelving books.

Fifteen minutes later Frog bounded into the library. *"Shhh!"* Ruthella put a finger on her lips.

Frog looked over at Miss Lemon. *"What?"* signed Frog. *"She's Deaf!"*

Frog signed *"Deaf"* by putting her index finger next to her ear and then next to the side of her mouth. *Deaf.*

"Miss Lemon can feel the floor vibrate!" signed Ruthella. *"She feels everything!"*

With great exaggeration, Frog tiptoed over to Charlie. She pulled out her notebook and pen. Charlie felt a surge of hope. It was time. Time to solve this mystery.

I've been thinking all night, wrote Frog, *because I keep feeling like there's something I've overlooked. This morning I realized what it was. I never asked you any questions about the knocking you heard. Why the knocking? Why NOW?*

Outside the library windows, thick dark clouds were filling the sky.

What's odd, wrote Frog, *is that Rupert never admitted to doing the knocking. Just like he never admitted to scaring Miss Tweedy and Millie with his fake bony hand. Why wouldn't he just say he did both of those things?*

That *was* odd, Charlie thought. Maybe Rupert hadn't admitted to the knocking or the scaring because he hadn't done them.

The knocking happened twice, right? wrote Frog.

"Yes," signed Charlie. *Once in the hallway when I was going to Grandpa Sol's study,* he wrote. *And once in the movie theater bathroom.*

What if someone was trying to send you a message? wrote Frog. *They knocked knowing you would hear it.*

That made sense to Charlie. But what was the message?

"*Do you remember the pattern?*" signed Frog.

"*I think so,*" he signed.

Charlie glanced over at Miss Lemon. He very softly knocked what he remembered hearing. First it was two short knocks, quick pause, one long knock. For the two short knocks, Charlie tapped his knuckles on the wooden table. For the long knock, he gently hit the table with his open hand.

Tap-tap, pound.

That was it.

Then it was: *tap-pound-pound,* then something, *tap-tap-tap.*

The last one was easy to remember: *pound-pound, tap.*

Charlie put it together:

Tap-tap, pound . . . tap-pound-pound something *tap-tap-tap . . . pound-pound, tap.*

He looked at Frog. He was knocking too softly for Frog to feel the vibration.

"Do it on my arm," signed Frog.

Charlie gently pounded and tapped out the message on Frog's forearm.

Frog drummed her fingers on the table, deep in thought. Then she paced quietly back and forth, twisting her long, glittery necklace.

"That's it," signed Frog.

"What's it?" asked Charlie.

Frog didn't answer. Instead she went over to where Miss Lemon was sleeping. There was a cabinet right next to her. Frog reached over and slowly opened the cabinet door.

Miss Lemon stopped snoring.

Frog pulled out a flashlight.

Miss Lemon opened her eyes.

Frog froze.

Charlie hoped Miss Lemon's eyesight was like those animals that saw you only if you moved. If you stayed still, they couldn't see you.

Frog was obviously thinking the same thing. She stood perfectly still next to Miss Lemon. Finally, Miss Lemon's eyes fluttered closed once more.

Frog tiptoed her way back to Charlie.

Remember, wrote Frog, *when your grandparents were in Herman's taxi and they beeped their horn AND flashed their light to get our attention?*

She handed the flashlight to Charlie.

"Show me the knocking pattern, but with the light this time," signed Frog.

Charlie flashed the light: quick, quick . . . slow.

Pause.

Quick, slow, slow . . . ? . . . quick, quick, quick.

Pause.

Slow, slow . . . quick.

"What are you doing?" signed Ruthella from the other side of the library.

"Detective work," signed Frog.

"Okay," signed Ruthella. If it wasn't about a book, she wasn't interested.

Frog grabbed the pen.

The person knocking, wrote Frog, *really WAS sending you a message!*

But what message? asked Charlie.

Frog went over to the library computer and typed something. She found what she wanted and went over to a shelf near the windows.

When Frog returned, she had a book with her: *Morse Code for Everyone.*

Charlie had heard of Morse code, but he had never used it before.

We use Morse code with the signal lamp, wrote Frog, *to communicate with Mr. Simple about the gondola. But Morse code can also be sent through sound.*

Frog opened the book and skimmed it. She pointed to a sentence in the book.

Morse code is a method of sending messages. It was originally created by Samuel F. B. Morse, along with other inventors in the 1800s, to work the telegraph.

Ruthella was getting ready to leave. She noticed their conversation. It was about a book, so now she was interested.

"Did you know," signed Ruthella, *"that Samuel Morse's second wife was Deaf? Her name was Sarah Elizabeth Griswold. Some people believed she helped her husband invent Morse code. And I read that sometimes they communicated to each other by tapping Morse code on each other's hands."*

"Wow!" signed Charlie and Frog. *"That was interesting."* Satisfied, Ruthella left the library.

Frog turned to the Morse code chart in the book, which showed how to communicate letters and words with sound or light signals. Each letter was made up of "dashes" or "dots." A dash was a longer signal, a dot a shorter signal. You paused briefly between letters. You paused slightly longer between words.

The letter *E* was the most often used letter in English, so it had the shortest flash of light or sound: just one single dot.

"Show me the message again," signed Frog.

Charlie flashed the light. Frog wrote down a dot or a dash, depending if Charlie flashed the light quickly or slowly. She drew a slanted line for a long pause. She wrote down a question mark for the part Charlie didn't remember.

.. - / .-- ? .../ -- .

Frog looked at the Morse code chart. She wrote out the corresponding letters:

IT W?S ME.

Frog added the letter *A* between the *W* and *S*.

IT WAS ME.

That was the message someone sent Charlie.

The flashlight rolled off the table and banged on the floor.

Miss Lemon's eyes popped open.

Morse Code

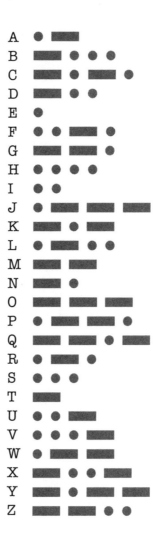

30. Stand

They should have dropped like stones, but instead they stood like statues.

Miss Lemon was staring right at them. Time slowed down. It slowed so much that Charlie had time to picture the sign for "*stand*" in his mind: you made the letter *V* and then turned it upside down on your other palm. *Stand.*

Miss Lemon had more wrinkles than Charlie had ever seen on one person. But her eyes were big and bright. Time sped up. Miss Lemon pointed to the flashlight and gestured for Charlie to give it to her.

Charlie gulped. He picked up the flashlight and handed it to Miss Lemon.

He hurried back to Frog, who still stood like a statue.

Miss Lemon fiddled with the on and off switch of the flashlight a few times.

Then she flashed it on purpose:

Quick, quick.

Pause.

Quick, quick, quick . . . quick . . . quick.

Pause.

Slow, quick, slow, slow . . . slow, slow, slow . . . quick, quick, slow.

Frog and Charlie looked at each other in surprise. Then Frog grabbed the pen. Miss Lemon flashed her light pattern once more. Frog wrote it down.

.. / ... . ./ -.-- --- ..-

Frog looked at the Morse code chart and wrote down the message:

I SEE YOU.

This was so unexpected that Charlie and Frog both laughed. Miss Lemon chuckled and closed her eyes again. Shaking their heads at this new view of Miss Lemon, they returned to the message Charlie had heard.

IT WAS ME.

Charlie softly knocked out the short taps and long

pounds to match those Morse code letters. That's what he had heard. That's exactly what he had heard.

"*Look at this,*" signed Frog. She wrote: *NO ONE SAW...* That was the message the Boney Hand had fingerspelled to the caretaker.

Right after it Frog wrote, *IT WAS ME.* That was the message someone had sent to Charlie.

When put together they fit perfectly.

NO ONE SAW IT WAS ME.

Frog's eyes grew wide.

Either it's the Boney Hand sending you this message, wrote Frog, *or it's the person who stole the Boney Hand, telling you "It was me."*

"*But why?*" signed Charlie. "*Why would the thief do that?*"

"*Guilt,*" signed Frog immediately. *The thief feels guilty*, she wrote. *Guilt is a great motive.*

Frog tapped the pen against her lips for a moment. *If it is a thief,* wrote Frog, *then we should send a message right back to him. Or her. We can do it at dinner, when most of the school is there.*

Charlie realized something. *If we're sending a message through knocking, like the thief did, then the thief has to be able to hear the message, right?*

Frog nodded. *But if the thief is completely deaf,* wrote Frog, *then we have to send the message with light—and that would attract too much attention.* Frog thought for a moment. *We'll just have to make sure the thief can FEEL the message we send,* wrote Frog. *But if the thief is hard of hearing, I have a guess who the thief might be.*

"*Who?*" signed Charlie.

JASPER, Frog fingerspelled.

Jasper, who was Deaf, but also hard of hearing.

Images of Jasper flashed in front of Charlie.

Jasper, being teased about smelling bad and not showering.

Jasper, standing alone after the Legend of the Boney Hand, not smiling or hugging anyone.

Jasper, hanging his head and looking hurt.

Jasper, rubbing his sore arm where he had just been punched.

Why was Jasper friends with someone like Rupert? Why didn't he stand up to him? Jasper was much bigger than Rupert. Perhaps Jasper was like Charlie when Charlie first met Rupert—he wanted Rupert to like him. Maybe Jasper had stolen the Boney Hand to impress Rupert and then felt guilty about it. Because maybe Jasper wanted Rupert to like him, but he didn't want to BE like Rupert. And that's why he was trying to confess.

Why don't we just ask Jasper? wrote Charlie.

Because, wrote Frog, *he might just deny it. Instead, we need to play his game. We need to send him a message.*

Charlie looked at Frog.

What message should we send? asked Charlie.

A message of justice! A message that says, "You stole the Boney Hand! You scared people with it! We know you did it! Confess or else!"

But, Frog, wrote Charlie, *if Jasper is trying to communicate with us, he wants us to understand something. We need to send a message that tells him we're TRYING to understand.*

We need to make him pay for what he did! wrote Frog.

First we need to understand why, Charlie wrote back.

Frog drummed her pen on the notebook and tucked a curl behind one ear. Eventually, she wrote: *Fine. What should we say?*

Charlie turned the page and pointed to Miss Lemon's Morse code message.

I SEE YOU.

• • •

A gusty wind whirled around the castle as dinner was served in the dining hall.

Millie was upstairs eating with her parents. Ruthella sat with Charlie and Frog, her nose buried in a book. They had chosen a table right next to Rupert and Jasper. As they ate, Charlie watched Rupert joke and tell stories. Jasper sat next to him, trying to eat but constantly getting poked in the ribs by Rupert.

Charlie and Frog's message was ready.

They were waiting until just before dinner was over. Then they would send it. Charlie hoped they were right. If they were, they would have the Boney Hand back tonight.

Everyone would know Frog had solved this case.

Everyone would know Charlie wasn't guilty.

Frog looked at the big clock and then at Charlie. They both looked at the Morse code message they had written out. They had shortened the message to make it easier to repeat.

A dot was a short tap. A dash was a long pound. Frog left a space in between letters. In between words Frog had drawn a slanted line.

.— — ./ ... . ./ ..—

Underneath the table, they each began to stomp on the wooden floor.

They hit the floor with just the ball of their foot for the dots and pounded their full foot on the floor for the dashes. They paused slightly between each letter. Between each word was a longer pause: *tap-pound-pound, tap . . . tap-tap-tap, tap, tap . . . tap-tap-pound.*

At first they stomped the floor softly, as if they were just playing a game. As students began clearing their plates, they stomped louder. Ruthella, feeling the vibrations, looked up.

It didn't have anything to do with a book, so Ruthella shrugged and went back to reading.

The few hearing people in the dining hall, like Boris, looked over. The few hard-of-hearing students, Jasper included, glanced over. Wendell refused to look because it was Charlie.

Don't worry, Wendell, Charlie thought. We'll have the Boney Hand back tonight.

Many of the other students, feeling the vibrations, asked what was going on.

"We're just playing a game," signed Frog.

Charlie and Frog continued to send their Morse code message until one of the cooks told them to stop.

Had their message been received? It was time to leave and see if the thief would follow them.

31. True

Frog had insisted they had to end this mystery where it started, inside the church cemetery. Drops of freezing rain fell on Charlie and Frog as they slowly walked, making sure whoever wanted to follow them could easily do so. This time Charlie didn't hesitate when they arrived at the graveyard door—he walked right in on the heels of Frog.

With her flashlight on, Frog led Charlie down the path to the stone church. Charlie used his own flashlight to watch the ground. He still felt spooked after being fooled by Rupert's fake hand.

What if they were wrong?

What if the Boney Hand hadn't been stolen? What if the Boney Hand was crawling around the graveyard right now?

They sat on the bench outside the church.

"*Now we wait,*" signed Frog. "*It's almost over. I can feel it.*"

Charlie hoped so. Because it certainly didn't feel safe sitting out here. And it was cold and wet. But being safe, warm, and dry were never Frog's primary concerns when there was a mystery to solve. Charlie was about to tell Frog they should sit inside the church, even if it would be harder for the thief to find them. They could leave a note on the door: *We're inside. Come on in, thief!*

Then, unbelievably, someone *was* walking toward them. Frog waited until the person was almost there, and then she swung her flashlight toward the suspect.

Oliver.

But Oliver wasn't the thief—Oliver was just being nosy.

"*What are you doing?*" signed Oliver. "*Why are you here?*"

"*Why are YOU here?*" signed Frog. "*Stop following us!*"

"*No problem,*" signed Oliver. "*Mom wanted me to find you. I'll just go back and let her know where you are.*" Oliver turned to leave.

Frog grabbed his arm. "*No! Stay!*"

Oliver paused and considered this.

"Only if you say please," signed Oliver.

"Please!!!" Charlie and Frog both signed.

"Okay," he signed cheerfully, obviously never planning to leave in the first place.

Charlie sat back down. Oliver sat next to him while Frog began to pace back and forth, twisting her necklace around and around. Her necklace was going to break with all the twisting she had been doing today.

"So what was all that pounding on the floor about?" Oliver asked Charlie. "Who were you telling 'We see you'?"

"You know Morse code?" asked Charlie.

"I work at the gondola sometimes," said Oliver. "You have to know it to work the signal light. Wow, it's cold out here."

"We were sending a message," said Charlie. "For the person who stole the Boney Hand."

"You know who did it?" asked Oliver.

"We think so," he said.

"Who?" asked Oliver.

Charlie didn't answer. He didn't want to say the thief's name until he showed up.

Oliver didn't press him. "I just hope something exciting happens," he said. "And that it doesn't start to pour."

"Will you interpret for me if I need it?" asked Charlie.

"What else have I got to do?"

"Thanks," said Charlie. "I owe you."

"I'll remember that, Charlie Tickler."

They waited and waited.

The wind and the rain blew harder.

They shivered and waited some more.

Time passed and nothing happened. Finally, Frog stopped pacing. As she turned on her flashlight to sign something, Charlie heard a twig snap.

He motioned to Frog to turn off the light. The footsteps grew closer and closer. A dark figure appeared on the path.

Frog aimed her flashlight toward the suspect and shined it in his face.

A great gust of wind blew. Leaves tumbled off the trees, spinning and falling to the ground.

It was Wendell.

• • •

It was Wendell Finch.

Wendell, who loved the story of Boney Jack.

Wendell, who would never do anything to hurt the memory of Boney Jack.

It was Wendell who walked toward Charlie, Frog, and Oliver. He was wearing a backpack.

"The Boney Hand?" signed Frog.

Wendell pointed to his backpack and nodded.

"*I got your message,*" signed Wendell. "*That means you got mine.*"

Wendell had been doing the knocking.

Wendell Finch.

"*I felt guilty,*" Wendell signed as Oliver interpreted, "*because Charlie was being blamed for taking the Boney Hand. I never meant for that to happen.*"

"*I knew it,*" signed Frog. "*Guilt will get you every time. But why? Why did you steal it?*"

Wendell kicked at the ground with the toe of one sneaker.

"*I saw Rupert,*" signed Wendell, "*right before the Legend of the Boney Hand performance. He told Jasper he was going to steal the hand and scare people with it. I just couldn't let that happen.*"

"*Maybe he was just joking,*" signed Frog.

"*He wasn't! He had that look he gets when he's about to do something really bad. And he was the one who unlocked the back door!*"

"*You should have told someone!*" signed Frog.

"*Who?*" signed Wendell. "*Who would have believed me? Grown-ups always believe Rupert is innocent.*"

Oliver added his own opinion.

"*True,*" Oliver signed by touching the side of his index finger to the front of his lips and then bringing his finger down.

Charlie had so many questions.

"How?" signed Charlie. *"How did you do it?"*

"I went in the back door of the church," Wendell signed as Oliver interpreted. *"I lifted the glass dome, but it was heavy. It slipped and fell. I knew you'd hear that, so I rolled under a pew. When you came in, the Boney Hand fell off the table. After you ran away, I grabbed the hand and ran out the back."*

"But you touched the Boney Hand!" signed Frog. *"You know what the legend says!"*

"I took off my jacket," signed Wendell, *"and wrapped the Boney Hand in it. Just like in the movie."*

"I knew it!" Frog signed again.

"Protecting the Boney Hand from a bully was more important to me than the curse!" signed Wendell. *"I would die for the Boney Hand!"*

"Well, you might just get your chance," Frog's hands snapped. She looked just like Mrs. Castle when she signed that.

"Boney Jack did good things for people," Wendell told her. *"But in the end, no one saw him as good. I thought I was doing something good by protecting the Boney Hand. But then Charlie was blamed! And I knew even if I returned the Boney Hand, people would still blame Charlie. And you, too, Frog,"* Wendell added. *"People would still think you made Charlie do it just to solve a case."*

"That's why you need to confess!" signed Frog.

"*I will*," Wendell signed. "*I'm going to confess to Mr. Willoughby that I stole the Boney Hand. It will be my last good deed at this school.*"

"*No!*" signed Charlie.

"*Yes!*" signed Frog.

"But Willoughby will get him expelled!" said Charlie as Oliver interpreted. "Wendell didn't do anything wrong! He was trying to do something right!"

"*If he doesn't admit taking it,*" signed Frog, "*then everyone who thinks you stole the Boney Hand will still think you did it. And everyone who thinks I convinced you to do it so that I could solve a case will still think that, too!*"

Charlie looked at Wendell, who seemed smaller than ever. It was true. If Wendell simply left the Boney Hand on the velvet pillow, everyone who believed Charlie had stolen it would simply think Charlie had returned it. He would still be blamed.

But Charlie couldn't control what everyone would think. He could only control what he thought.

"*Good people do good things,*" Charlie reminded Frog as rain fell out of the clouds like a bucket upended.

• • •

The four of them rushed into the church.

They stood in the vestibule, their clothes soaking wet. Dim lights illuminated the sanctuary. From inside the entranceway, Charlie could see the pedestal at the front of the church, with its red velvet pillow on top.

Its empty red velvet pillow.

"Good people do good things," Frog repeated, as if talking to herself. She pushed her wet, curly hair out of her face and looked right at Wendell. She waited for him to take off his glasses, wipe them, and then put them back on.

"You did something good," signed Frog. She hesitated and then added, *"You shouldn't get in trouble because of that."*

"Whoa," Oliver whispered. "Miracles really do happen."

"Put the hand back," Frog told Wendell. *"We won't say anything."*

"Really?" signed Wendell. *"Are you sure?"*

Charlie and Frog looked at each and then at Wendell. *"We're sure,"* they signed.

Wendell took off his backpack and gently placed it on the vestibule floor. Charlie, Frog, and Oliver all took a step backward. Wendell unzipped it, reached inside, and pulled out a rolled-up fleece jacket. He placed that on top of the backpack.

Frog and Oliver shuddered.

Slowly Wendell unfurled the coat.

All of them drew back at the sight of the yellow-brown Boney Hand. It was a frightening thing to see outside its glass enclosure. Fingers curled, it looked ready to leap up and grab any one of them.

"*Isn't it beautiful?*" signed Wendell. "*I can't believe I stole it.*"

"*I can't either,*" signed Charlie.

"*Are you sure I should do this?*" asked Wendell.

"We're sure," Charlie and Frog signed again.

Wendell reached into his pocket and pulled out a pair of gloves. He put them on and braved death again as he carefully picked up the Boney Hand.

Frog and Oliver shuddered once more.

Wendell took a few moments to gaze at Boney Jack's hand one last time before he returned it.

"*This will be the second case we've solved,*" Frog signed to Charlie, "*and once again we can't tell anyone.*"

Wendell took a deep breath and was just about to take his first step into the church when Frog stopped him.

"*Don't do it!*" signed Frog.

32. Idea

Charlie, Oliver, and Wendell stared at Frog. Was she changing her mind? But Frog was pointing to the front of the church.

"Look," signed Frog.

Up in the corner, near the roof, was a small camera. It was aimed directly at the pedestal. As they watched, a small red light blinked on and off.

"That's a time-lapse camera," signed Frog. *"Boris has one just like it. I knew we couldn't trust Willoughby!"*

Mr. Willoughby had spread the word that no one would be punished if the thief returned the Boney Hand. But secretly he had mounted a camera to catch the thief.

"*I don't think,*" signed Frog, "*that the camera can see all the way in the back of the church. At least, I hope it can't.*" She turned to Wendell. "*We'll have to leave the hand somewhere else so you aren't caught on camera.*"

"*No.*" Wendell shook his head. "*I have to return the hand back to where I took it from. I have to be respectful to the memory of Boney Jack!*"

Wendell had a stubborn look upon his face, not unlike the one Frog often had.

"*I'm going to put it back,*" Wendell told them as Oliver interpreted. "*Boney Jack walked the plank for his good deeds. This is my plank.*"

Wendell squared his narrow shoulders and stepped forward. Frog yanked him back into the vestibule. Wendell almost dropped the Boney Hand. Charlie and Oliver both stifled screams as Wendell caught it just in time.

Frog hadn't noticed. She was staring up at the camera.

"*I have a better idea,*" signed Frog.

Frog made the letter *I*. She touched her pinky finger to the side of her forehead, palm facing inward. Then she drew her pinky finger forward. *Idea.*

"*Look at your watch,*" Frog told Charlie. "*How much time is between the light flashes?*"

Charlie held up his watch with the screen illuminated. When the red light blinked, Charlie started counting seconds. When it blinked again, Charlie stopped.

"*Ten seconds,*" signed Charlie.

"*That means we have ten seconds between camera shots,*" signed Frog, "*to make it look like the Boney Hand crawled up the church aisle and onto the pillow. If the camera has already seen us, then it's too late. But if it hasn't, we have a chance.*"

When it dawned on Wendell what Frog wanted to do, his eyes brightened behind his round glasses.

Charlie looked down the long church aisle, where the pedestal stood. Someone would have to run up and down the aisle, placing the Boney Hand in position every ten seconds without getting caught on camera.

"*So,*" Frog asked, "*who's the fastest?*"

"*Not me,*" signed Oliver. "*I'm strong, not fast.*"

But Frog was looking at Charlie.

Charlie, who was on the track team.

Charlie, who had been practicing running fast.

"*It's me,*" signed Charlie. "*I'm the fastest. I'll do it.*"

"But," said Oliver, "if you don't time the camera right, you'll be caught. Then everyone will really think you're the thief!" Oliver signed what he had just said for Frog and Wendell.

"*It'll work,*" signed Charlie. He didn't know if it really would—but he had to try.

Wendell placed the Boney Hand down on the jacket and took off his gloves. Charlie removed his shoes so he wouldn't leave muddy footprints on the church floor. He took off his watch and handed it to Frog. Then he put on Wendell's gloves.

He hesitated.

"We don't know if gloves will protect you," Frog warned. *"Are you sure?"*

Charlie looked at Wendell, who had been brave enough to protect the Boney Hand from Rupert in the first place.

Charlie nodded. He was sure.

Charlie reached down and lifted up the hand.

Frog and Oliver both shuddered again.

Charlie held it away from his body and tried not to look at it.

They all watched the red light flash. Heart thudding, Charlie placed the Boney Hand in the aisle a few feet inside the church. He dashed back to the entrance hall. The light flashed again. He took another ten seconds to calm his heart rate.

The light blinked. Charlie picked up the Boney Hand and moved it a few feet forward. He darted back.

Ten more seconds.

Charlie moved the Boney Hand farther and farther up the aisle, each time barreling back to the entrance before the next picture snapped. The closer the Boney

Hand moved toward the pedestal, the quicker Charlie had to run. He was breathing hard now.

"*Couldn't Charlie just duck down between the pews?*" Oliver asked Frog.

"*The camera is so high up,*" signed Frog, "*that it still might see Charlie.*"

The camera flashed again.

"*Hurry,*" signed Frog.

Charlie sprinted as fast as he could, picked up the Boney Hand, placed it right in front of the pedestal, and sprinted back, almost tripping over his feet. He made it back just before the light blinked again.

Heart hammering, Charlie put his hands on his knees and tried to catch his breath. But there was no time to think. He had to run—soon—and fast! He had to pick up the Boney Hand, put it on the pillow on the pedestal, and tear back down the aisle before the camera blinked again.

Without tripping.

Without dropping the Boney Hand.

Coach Crawford said to visualize yourself going through the race. Charlie pictured himself running with great, long strides. He saw himself picking up the Boney Hand and placing it on the pillow. He imagined himself turning around easily and then taking great, long strides back.

He waited for the light.

It blinked.

Nope, he wasn't ready.

Charlie got into his runner's stance, like he would for a track meet.

The light blinked.

Nope. Still not ready.

Frog, Oliver, and Wendell all patted him on his back.

This time Charlie was ready.

The light blinked.

Go!

Charlie ran harder than he had ever run before. He scooped up the Boney Hand in one smooth, fluid movement. He put it on the pillow and spun around in the same breath.

Oliver and Wendell looked terrified as Frog frantically pointed at his watch. All of them were waving their arms at him, begging him to move faster.

Charlie careened down the aisle. He took great leaping strides as he watched Frog's fingers count down.

Three.

Charlie pumped his arms.

Two.

Charlie was flying.

One.

Charlie dove through the air right into the arms of Frog, Oliver, and Wendell.

The camera light blinked.

Charlie had made it.

33. Proud

By the time Charlie rode the gondola back to the village, it had stopped raining. Grandma and Grandpa Tickler were at the kitchen table with Yvette when Charlie walked through the door, ready to play their favorite card game, Kings Corners.

"Charlie! We're so glad you're home!" said Grandma.

"Ayuh," said Grandpa.

"So am I," said Yvette. "Because now I don't have to play."

"You have to play, Yvette!" said Grandma. "It's more fun with more players."

As Yvette dealt cards (seven cards to each player, the

right number), Grandma Tickler asked, "How's our first case coming along? The Mystery of the Disappearing Boney Hand?"

Charlie picked up his cards. He had two high cards, a king and queen.

"We solved it," said Charlie. "We know who stole the Boney Hand."

"You do?" said Grandma. "Well, how about that!"

Charlie figured it was safe to tell his grandparents some of what happened as they didn't know much ASL and had only been to the castle once. They were unlikely to tell anyone at CSD the real story. So he told them how Frog had figured out that Charlie was being sent a message. How he and Frog had sent a message in return. And how the thief turned out to be a boy who simply wanted to protect the Boney Hand from a bully.

"So he was doing something good!" said Grandma. "Something good that looked bad."

"Ayuh!" said Grandpa.

"That's right, Irving," said Grandma. "You can't always know if someone is good or bad just by what you see. We learned that with Walter Simple, didn't we?"

They played two more hands of cards before Grandma looked at the kitchen clock. "Irving, *Vince Vinelli Special Edition!* is starting! Charlie, I'm glad you and Frog solved the case. But don't forget—the Mystery

of the Missing Remote Control, the Mystery of the
Frozen Underwear, and the Mystery of the Stolen Black
Jelly Beans are still unsolved!"

Grandpa patted Charlie's head and shuffled into the
living room behind Grandma.

Charlie started to get up, too.

"Hold on," said Yvette. She picked up the cards on
the table. "What's going to happen to that boy?" she
asked as she cut the deck of cards with one hand. "Is he
going to be in trouble?"

"If I tell you," said Charlie, "you have to promise not
to tell anyone. Ever."

"Promise," said Yvette. She was shuffling cards, so
her fingers were not crossed.

Charlie told Yvette about Mr. Willoughby and the
camera, and how Charlie had moved the Boney Hand
so that it looked like it crawled down the church aisle
on its own.

"But we don't know if it worked," said Charlie. "I
could've been caught on camera."

"And if you were caught on camera, people will think
you had something to do with stealing the hand, since
you were the one returning it," said Yvette.

Charlie nodded.

"You could have just turned Wendell in and cleared
your name," added Yvette.

Charlie nodded again.

Yvette leaned back in her chair and gave Charlie a long, considering look.

"It takes a special kind of strength," said Yvette, "to not let what other people might think keep you from doing the right thing. I'm proud of you, Charlie Tickler."

Charlie ducked his head. In his mind's eye he signed *"proud"* by making a thumbs-down and then sliding his thumb up his chest. *Proud.*

"Thanks," he said. "You should be proud of Frog, too," added Charlie. "She wanted to prove to everyone she was a real detective, especially after what Vince Vinelli said. But she won't tell anyone she solved this case, because of Wendell."

"That's real strength," said Yvette. "Strength of character."

"I told Frog we'd make sure everyone knows about the next mystery we solve—if I'm not expelled," said Charlie.

Yvette cut the deck of cards with one hand. "How do you do that?" Charlie asked Yvette.

"Lots of practice," said Yvette. "Here, I'll show you."

She slowed down what she was doing so Charlie could see how her fingers held some of the cards while moving the other half of the cards. Then she gave the deck to Charlie. He tried to cut the cards with one hand. They scattered all over the table.

"Keep trying," said Yvette as she collected the cards and handed them back to Charlie. "That's the only way to get good at something."

Charlie tried to cut the cards with one hand. Once again, he failed. Yvette gathered them up.

"Frog already knows what she wants to be good at," said Charlie. "That's why she's doing detective work now. Oliver already knows, too. That's why he bakes all the time. But I have no idea what I want to do when I grow up."

"You don't have to know right now," said Yvette. She laid the cards in a long line and flipped them over as one. Then she scooped them up and handed them back to Charlie. "Plenty of people don't know what makes them happy until they're already all grown up and living their lives. You've got lots of time to figure it out."

Charlie felt relieved that he didn't have to know right now. In the meantime, he had lots of stuff he wanted to do—like learn more ASL, run faster, and cut a deck of cards one-handed like Yvette. Charlie tried once more. The cards slipped, but they didn't fall. He caught them with his other hand and tried again.

"Your grandparents just now found something that makes them happy," said Yvette as she watched Charlie practice. "Solving crime. Wonder when they're going to solve their three cases," she said, giving him a sideways look.

"Yvette!" said Charlie. "You didn't!"

Yvette went over to a kitchen cabinet and opened it. She pulled out the remote control from behind the flour canister, along with a jar of black jelly beans.

"Oh, yes I did," said Yvette. She tucked the remote control and jelly beans back behind the flour. "I knew your grandparents weren't going to be much help to you finding the Boney Hand. They needed some mysteries of their own to solve. The missing remote control gets them out of their chairs when they're watching TV. When I was folding laundry, I decided to toss a pair of Irving's briefs in the freezer, just to see if they noticed. And Irving needs to eat more than one color of jelly beans!"

"But you told them you didn't do it!" said Charlie. "Each time they asked you, you said it wasn't you!"

"I never said that," said Yvette. "I said, 'Why would I take the remote control?' 'Why would I freeze Irving's underwear?' 'Why would I take black jelly beans?' I answered a question with a question. Then I distracted them."

"Smart," said Charlie.

"I wasn't born yesterday," said Yvette as she shuffled cards. "We'll give your grandparents a few more days of investigating, then let's figure out a way for them to solve these cases."

34. Egg

Charlie wondered if today would be his last day at Castle School for the Deaf.

The day seemed perfect—the sky was so blue, the autumn leaves so vivid, the houses so colorful—that it made what Charlie was feeling inside that much worse. He could, of course, continue to live with his grandparents and go to the local school, but it wouldn't be the same.

As Charlie lined up for the gondola, he realized everyone was talking about one subject: the Boney Hand. Bits and pieces of conversations floated all around him, in ASL and in English.

"I heard they found it!"

"I heard that, too!"

"*Who took it?*"

"*No idea!*"

"*Did it come back on its own? That's what someone told me.*"

"This village and castle aren't normal—that's what I love about them—anything can happen here!"

The gondola returned to the village side of the river. Mr. Simple came out of the control station to load passengers and collect a dollar from each rider.

"I didn't steal the Boney Hand," said Mr. Simple as Charlie handed him his fare.

"I know," said Charlie.

"The rumor is it's back," said Mr. Simple. "Who brought it back?"

"We'll find out, I guess," said Charlie, feeling sick to his stomach.

"If it came back on its own," said Mr. Simple, "it didn't ride in my gondola." He turned to the next passenger to collect a dollar, and then added, "I wouldn't put up with a bony hand riding my gondola for free."

• • •

The Flying Hands Café was packed. Frog was rushing around taking and serving orders. Mrs. Castle was seating customers. Every few minutes, she checked her phone. Charlie slipped into the café when Mrs. Castle's back was turned. He went over to Frog's section.

Frog was taking an order for eggs from a man who was obviously new to ASL. He slowly made the letter *H* with both hands, putting one *H* on top of the other one. Then he broke them apart like an egg cracking open. *Egg.*

Frog gave him a thumbs-up and wrote down the order. She spotted Charlie. Pulling him aside, she quickly scribbled on her notepad, her thick jeweled bracelet sliding down her arm.

Willoughby found the Boney Hand in the church early this morning, wrote Frog. *Now he's watching the camera recording. Mom is waiting to hear from him. Mom, Dad, and Grandpa were* NOT *happy about the camera.*

Charlie felt queasy. He must have looked it, too, because Frog pulled him over to a family's table. There was one extra chair. She pushed Charlie into it. The family looked surprised, but they were obviously hearing and didn't know how to sign *"What are you doing?"* They shrugged and went back to their pancakes.

Don't worry, wrote Frog. *It'll be fine. I'll bring you some breakfast. No charge.*

Frog had never offered Charlie free food before. She must not have a good feeling about this. She must think last night didn't work. That Mr. Willoughby was going to see Charlie on the camera.

Charlie watched the family he was sitting with trying to communicate by fingerspelling.

Mother: EAT!

Little girl: NO!

Father (pointing to his pancakes): GOOD!

Frog brought Charlie eggs and banana bread. *The banana bread is from Oliver*, wrote Frog. *You get the first taste!*

Charlie looked over and saw Oliver give him a wave and a thumbs-up from the kitchen.

He didn't like everyone being so nice to him. He didn't like it at all. It meant they were sure Charlie was going to get caught. Well, what if he did? He would just say he hadn't stolen the hand, and he wouldn't say who did.

But then Mr. Willoughby would ask, "Why were you returning it? What's in it for you?"

And what was Charlie supposed to say? "I was trying to do something good"?

Mr. Willoughby would not believe him.

No one would believe him.

The banana bread looked delicious, but Charlie couldn't eat it.

He saw Mrs. Castle look at her phone and put her hand on her chest.

This was it.

Mrs. Castle signed something to the woman next to her and then hurried out of the café.

Frog was at Charlie's side in an instant.

"Let's go," she signed.

· · ·

Mrs. Castle must have texted Grandpa Sol because he was with her as they walked to the graveyard. Charlie and Frog waited a moment so they would not be seen, and then followed.

When they arrived at the cemetery entrance, they found Mr. Castle sitting on a stool by the wooden door, reading. Boris was leaning against the stone wall watching something on his phone.

"Sorry, Frog. Sorry, Charlie," Mr. Castle signed as Boris interpreted. *"I have strict orders not to let anyone in. I've been turning away students and visitors."*

"Dad! Please!" Frog begged.

Mr. Castle shook his head.

"Then at least tell us what you know!" signed Frog.

"I know nothing more than you do," he signed. *"I'm usually the last to know, anyway, so I just wait for the facts to come in."*

Frog looked at Boris.

Boris shrugged.

She threw up her hands in frustration and began to pace.

"Charlie," said Mr. Castle, "I never did get a chance

to tell you about my other theatrical experiences I had when I was your age. This is a perfect time for you to hear more of my stories!"

Mr. Castle switched to ASL. His story was a long one and took many detours. As Boris interpreted, Charlie could only think about what Mr. Willoughby was seeing on the camera right now.

As Frog paced back and forth, her father told the story of auditioning for the school play. Mr. Castle was signing, *"And then I said, 'But I don't want to be the White Rabbit—I want to be the Mad Hatter,'"* when the graveyard door opened.

35. Great!

Frog stopped pacing and grabbed Charlie's hand.

Grandpa Sol came out first. He saw Charlie and Frog, but his face remained expressionless.

Mr. Willoughby came out next. He looked right at them. Charlie waited to be told, "I saw you on camera." He waited to be told, "You will have to leave our school."

Frog clutched Charlie's hand.

But Mr. Willoughby's eyes never focused on them.

Instead, he seemed to be in a daze.

"Do you know what this means?" Mr. Willoughby signed to Grandpa Sol as Boris interpreted. *"This means I'm going to have to write a whole new script for our performance."*

"*Absolutely,*" signed Grandpa Sol. "*We have a new twist to our old legend. I have a feeling many people will want to attend the Legend of the Boney Hand just to see this unexpected ending.*"

"*I'll have to schedule more than just two performances,*" signed Mr. Willoughby. "*That means I'll need more actors!*"

"*So it would seem,*" agreed Grandpa Sol.

"*And I really think,*" Mr. Willoughby added as he and Grandpa Sol walked away, "*we are going to want costumes for everyone, not just me—although I'll certainly need a new one. And we need advertising! Perhaps we should hire a publicist?*"

Frog spun around to face Charlie and stared at him in disbelief.

It had worked.

It had really worked!

Charlie wanted to sign, "*Pah! We did it!*"

He could see Frog wanted to sign it, too, but they both caught themselves, remembering Boris and Mr. Castle were there.

"*Now, Charlie, where was I?*" signed Mr. Castle before noticing Mrs. Castle was motioning for Charlie, Frog, and Boris to come into the graveyard. Charlie's excited feeling fell away as they entered. Mrs. Castle signed something to her husband, who nodded and settled back on his stool with his book. Mrs. Castle shut the graveyard door.

"*So,*" she signed as Boris interpreted, "*the Boney Hand is back.*"

"*It is?*" signed Frog. She stared at her mother with wide eyes and an open mouth, appearing dumbfounded by this news. Frog should be an actor, not a detective. Frog made the sign "*great*" by placing her hands out in front of her—palms facing out, fingers pointing up—and pushing them forward and back. Then she lowered her hands and pushed them forward again.

"*That's great!*" signed Frog. "*Well, I need to get back to the café—*"

"*Apparently,*" continued Mrs. Castle as if Frog hadn't signed anything, "*Mr. Willoughby mounted a camera inside the church without our knowledge.*"

Mrs. Castle paused and looked at Boris, who kept a poker face and waited for her to continue. "*Mr. Willoughby believed whoever stole the Boney Hand was a student, and that the student would return it,*" she signed. "*But it seems the Boney Hand did not need someone to return it. It came back on its own. At first we weren't sure what we were seeing. But it's right there on the camera.*"

"*It's hard to believe!*" signed Frog. "*But I guess we HAVE to believe it! The legend is really true!*"

Mrs. Castle simply looked at Frog with a steady gaze.

"*Mom, I promise,*" signed Frog. "*I had nothing to do with stealing the Boney Hand.*"

Mrs. Castle's gaze slid over to Charlie.

"*I promise,*" signed Charlie, "*that I had nothing to do with stealing the Boney Hand.*"

Mrs. Castle nodded. "*I believe you,*" she signed. "*Both of you.*"

With a thumbs-up and a confident nod, Frog walked backward until she was pressed up against the graveyard door. "*And now I better go finish serving breakfast! Come on, Charlie!*" Frog opened the door and dashed out of the cemetery.

Charlie started to leave, too, but he wasn't quick enough.

"*Charlie,*" signed Mrs. Castle as Boris spoke. "*While the Boney Hand was missing, there was talk about you being an outsider.*" Mrs. Castle looked straight into Charlie's eyes. "*You are not an outsider.*"

"*But I'm hearing,*" signed Charlie. "*And I don't sign very well.*"

"*I don't see you as a hearing child who doesn't sign very well,*" Mrs. Castle told him. "*I see Charlie. I see you.*"

Relief flooded through Charlie.

It didn't matter to Mrs. Castle that he was hearing. That was all Charlie needed to know.

"*I just wish I knew more ASL,*" he signed. "*I'm learning as fast as I can.*"

"*And you'll keep learning,*" signed Mrs. Castle. "*But learning ASL doesn't begin here.*" She pointed to Charlie's hands. "*It begins here.*" She pointed to Charlie's heart. "*I*

*can't teach that. A student must already have that inside—
like you have."*

Charlie didn't fully understand what Mrs. Castle was
saying—but he *felt* what Mrs. Castle was saying.

And it felt good.

"Who else," signed Mrs. Castle, *"should I check with?
Just to make sure that everything is okay?"*

"Just to make sure they're okay?" asked Charlie.
"That's all?"

"Just to make sure they're okay," she repeated.

"Check on Jasper Dill," signed Charlie. *"I think he
needs someone to talk to."*

Charlie thought of someone else.

"And check on Rupert Miggs," signed Charlie. "Rupert is
not what he looks like," Charlie told Mrs. Castle as Boris
signed. "Grown-ups always see him as nice. He's not nice."

Mrs. Castle nodded and gave Charlie one of her
strong, solid hugs with the humming sound. Then she
signed her *"I'm-here-if-you-need-me"* sign. Charlie knew
that sign wasn't just for him. Mrs. Castle was there for
all of her students.

Even Rupert Miggs.

• • •

"I have no idea what just happened," said Boris as they
headed toward the castle. "But I always knew you and

Frog were a good team. You two are like Holmes and Watson! Dorrie and Jack!"

"You've read the Dorrie McCann books?" asked Charlie, incredulous.

"Hasn't everyone?" said Boris.

Charlie had made it through one book. That was enough.

"It's kind of cool," Boris continued, "to watch this new story become part of the legend. Stories are powerful, dude. That's why I love movies. And just for the record, I had no idea why Willoughby was grilling me about my time-lapse camera. You have to believe me."

"I believe you," said Charlie.

"Good," said Boris. He took a long look around the castle grounds. "When I finish film school, I'm coming back to make a sequel to *The Boney Hand*—I'll call it *The Boney Hand Returns!*"

Charlie saw Obie and Max sitting outside the barn, their faces tilted toward the morning sun. He knew Obie would soon be collecting different perspectives on what happened. Charlie wanted to tell him his version. He was sure Frog would agree that Obie, as caretaker of the castle, should know the truth. Obie was a secret-keeper. He wouldn't tell.

"How long is film school?" Charlie asked.

"A couple of years," said Boris.

"Then I'll still be here when you come back," said Charlie happily as he walked toward the barn.

• • •

During lunch outside, students were excitedly discussing this new development of the Legend of the Boney Hand. Charlie and Frog sat on a blanket spread over the still-damp ground, and watched Millie play catch with Bear and Boris. Wendell sat with them, watching everyone talk about his favorite person, Boney Jack. Wendell seemed delighted to have helped create this new piece of the famous legend.

Rupert ate lunch with Jasper, doing his usual joking and laughing. But for some reason, he left Charlie and Frog alone.

Bear caught the ball. This time, instead of bringing it to Millie or Boris, he brought it over to Jasper and dropped it at his feet. Bear's long pink tongue was hanging out of his mouth as he panted and waited for Jasper to throw the ball.

Millie came over.

"Do you want to play with us?" Millie signed to Jasper.

Jasper quickly looked at Rupert, as if asking permission.

Charlie had always thought Jasper was strong because his body was strong. Now he realized that being strong on the outside didn't necessarily mean you were strong on the inside.

Rupert didn't sign anything, but his mocking smile

said, "Why would you want to play ball with a little girl and her dog?"

In that moment, something seemed to shift within Jasper. He shrugged as if to say, "I don't care what you think."

Jasper picked up the ball. He almost smiled as he threw it. Bear galloped after it. Rupert turned to find someone to say something mean about Jasper. But for once, no one was interested. Rupert went back to eating his lunch. Alone.

Charlie studied Rupert from across the lawn. Without Jasper at his side, Rupert seemed smaller. Deflated. Charlie wondered what the other pieces of Rupert's puzzle were. He supposed he'd have to ask a lot of questions to find out.

Something occurred to him: Someone who gave out that much meanness must have a lot of meanness inside him to give. And that meanness had to come from somewhere. Where did it come from?

Chief Paley left the castle. She was heading toward the gondola landing when she spotted Charlie and Frog. She waved them over.

"*Sorry,*" signed Chief Paley.

"*Sorry about what?*" Charlie and Frog both asked.

"*Sorry,*" the chief signed, "*that you didn't solve the case.*"

The chief took out her notepad and wrote: *The missing Boney Hand case would have been great for you to solve. We'll never know what really happened now that the hand* is back, because Sol said the case is closed. *But I always suspected that kid.* She tipped her head toward Rupert. *He's a sycophant.*

"*A what?*" Charlie and Frog both signed, looking at that new word.

A sycophant, wrote the chief. *A lickspittle, a toady, a flatterer—someone who kisses up to adults so they think he's a good kid when he's not!*

Chief Paley had no problem seeing Rupert clearly. But Charlie knew that was only one piece of Rupert. It wasn't the whole puzzle.

"*Well, I'd better get going,*" signed Chief Paley. "*I need to tell Bone—*" Chief Paley stopped signing.

"*Tell Bone what?*" asked Frog.

"*Nothing,*" signed the chief.

Frog gave Chief Paley her best Frog look, which not even Chief Paley could withstand.

Okay, wrote the chief, *I'll tell you, but you can't tell anyone else.*

Charlie and Frog both nodded.

Bone is writing a history of the Boney Hand, wrote Chief Paley. *He's embarrassed to admit it because he has railed against the hand for so long. But it's his passion. And now he has a phenomenal ending for his book.*

What were you and Miss Tweedy doing with Bone, asked Frog, *the night the Boney Hand scared her?*

That's our weekly writing group, wrote Chief Paley.

Bone is writing his history book; I'm writing a mystery with a brilliant chief of police in a small, quirky village. And Miss Tweedy is writing, well, I'm not sure what Miss Tweedy is writing.

The chief saw the gondola approaching the castle and waved good-bye. Charlie saw Mrs. Castle and the man with paint-splattered clothes. They were setting up paint easels overlooking the Hudson River. Mrs. Castle was smiling.

Charlie pointed them out to Frog.

"I know!" signed Frog. *"I forgot to tell you!"* She gestured to Charlie for his pen and notebook that he always had in his back pocket. *That's Mr. Cole!* wrote Frog. *Remember Miss Tweedy mentioned him? He just opened an art studio in the village. Mom has always wanted to paint.*

But why did your mom look so anxious, asked Charlie, *when she saw him the morning of the Fall Extravaganza?*

Mr. Cole had come to the castle, Frog told him, *to convince Mom she could paint. Mom thought she couldn't paint because she wasn't good at it. Mr. Cole told her if she loved painting then she just had to start. He said often you have to paint badly before you can paint well.*

Charlie thought about what Yvette had said to him, that it might take a long time to find what makes you happy.

Mrs. Castle was finding that now.

36. Book

When Charlie arrived home from school, his grand-parents were asleep in their E-Z chair recliners. Charlie was glad—he needed a break. Grandparents were a lot of work.

Yvette was upstairs vacuuming. Charlie got an apple from the refrigerator. There was a stack of books on the table with a receipt from Blythe and Bone Bookshop— the books his parents had ordered before they left. Mr. Simple must have delivered them.

"*Book*" was an easy sign to remember: you put your palms together and then opened them up like a book.

Charlie looked at the titles. He wondered if Matilda

had helped his parents pick them. One book was called *How to Have a Good Life Even If Your Parents Weren't Good.* Another was *Parents Are Human Beings, Too.* A third was *Parenting Is Hard; Being a Child Is Harder.*

It suddenly occurred to Charlie that his parents were not only parents; they had also been children once, too. Charlie's mom's parents had died when she was a baby. But Charlie's father's parents were Grandma and Grandpa Tickler. What must it have been like to have them as parents?

Charlie picked up the book *Parents Are Human Beings, Too* and turned to the first page.

. . .

Just before dinner, the phone rang. Charlie was still reading at the kitchen table while Yvette was mashing potatoes. Charlie went to the black phone on the wall and answered it.

"Tickler residence, Charlie speaking."

"It's me, your mother!" said Mrs. Tickler.

"And me, your father!" added Mr. Tickler.

"Guess what, Mom and Dad?" he said. "The Boney Hand is back!"

"Oh, wonderful!" said Mrs. Tickler. "We're so relieved!"

"Indeed we are!" said Mr. Tickler.

Charlie glanced at the book in his hand. It was hard to think of his parents as people and not just parents. As Charlie had been reading, he realized there were many things about his parents he didn't know. He only saw the parent piece of his parents' puzzle.

So Charlie asked a question.

"Mom and Dad, how are you able to go all over the world and help animals? Isn't that expensive?"

"It is," said Mr. Tickler. "So we ask people for money to send us places."

"And they give us money," said Mrs. Tickler, "because we're very skilled at observing and understanding animals. We're excellent at watching them and collecting information about them. The more information we have, the more we can help them."

Charlie had never thought about his parents being smart with animals or smart about asking people for money. He had never thought his parents were smart about anything.

"But you can't just learn about animals from a book," said Charlie. "You have to watch them in their natural habitat. Right?"

"Of course!" said Mr. Tickler. "That's the only way to do it properly."

Mr. Tickler said this matter-of-factly, as if it were

the most obvious thing in the world. Charlie wondered why his mother and father couldn't see other obvious things as clearly as they saw animals.

Why couldn't they see Charlie?

A stab of anger burned inside him.

He was only a kid.

Why should Charlie have to tell his parents something they should already know?

But he had to. So he would.

"Mom and Dad," said Charlie, "did you know kids are a lot like animals? We're like blind salamanders or giant golden moles. We need to be observed in our natural habitat."

Yvette was mashing potatoes furiously while nodding her head furiously.

"Alistair, did you hear what Charlie said?" asked his mother.

"I certainly did, Myra," said his father. There was a long pause. Then he softly said, "I have never thought about children that way before."

Charlie swallowed. It hurt to swallow because of the thick lump that filled his throat. "Well," said Charlie, "that's how you figure out the parenting stuff. That's how you learn to be my mom and dad. But you can't learn that from books," he explained, his voice cracking just the tiniest bit.

"You have to be here," Charlie added, "to see me."

37. Strong

Charlie and Frog leaned against D.J. McKinnon's head-stone. Tapping the pen against her lips, Frog thought about what to write on her frog stationery. She wore a green-jeweled frog brooch that Wendell had given her from Junk and Stuff. Wendell had given Charlie an IOU for a triple ice cream cone from Nathan's Ice Cream Emporium.

Charlie and Frog both thought they received the better gift.

Frog began writing her letter to Vince Vinelli. After a few minutes, she paused and looked up.

"Did you ever think," Frog asked Charlie, *"that I wasn't really a detective? That I was just cute?"*

Charlie looked at Frog in surprise.

"Never," he signed.

Frog grinned.

It was Charlie's turn to ask the question he had wanted to ask since the Boney Hand went missing.

"Did you ever think I stole the Boney Hand?" asked Charlie.

Frog snorted.

"You?" she signed. *"Never."*

Charlie grinned.

Frog went back to writing her letter. Charlie let his head rest against the cool headstone. Today it felt peaceful in the graveyard. And, for once, not scary.

One thing, though, still mystified Charlie.

When Frog stopped writing again, Charlie wrote, *Rupert likes to brag about mean things he does. Why didn't he just admit that he scared Miss Tweedy and Millie with his fake bony hand?*

Maybe, Frog wrote, *he didn't brag about it because he didn't do it.*

If he didn't do it, then who did? asked Charlie. *Wendell did the knocking, but Wendell would never scare anyone, even if he did have the Boney Hand!*

Wendell wouldn't do that, agreed Frog. *But there's still another possibility. One that we considered at the beginning of our investigation.*

It dawned on Charlie what Frog meant.

"*You think the Boney Hand did it,*" signed Charlie. "*You think the Boney Hand got out of Wendell's backpack and scared them.*"

"*I'm just saying we don't know!*" signed Frog before returning to her writing.

Charlie realized Frog didn't *want* to know. She preferred that some things be left a mystery—like the Legend of the Boney Hand.

But now Charlie didn't feel as relaxed as he had a minute ago. He scanned the graveyard with watchful eyes, making sure a hand wasn't scuttling and scurrying around.

Frog finished her letter. She handed it to Charlie.

Dear Vince Vinelli,

This is Francine Castle, also known as Frog—that's Frog, not Froggy. I wrote you a letter, which you read on your show. I told you that I want to become a detective, but I actually have already started my detective career. My partner and I have solved two cases so far. Unfortunately, I am not at liberty to discuss them. But even though no one else knows we solved these mysteries, we know we solved them.

Because sometimes what you know on the inside is more important than what others see on the outside.

Sincerely,
Frog Castle

"*It's a good letter,*" signed Charlie as he handed it back to her.

Frog wrote one more thing at the bottom.

PS: I am not little or cute. If you need a word to describe me, you can call me—

"*I don't know what word to pick,*" signed Frog.

Charlie remembered what Yvette had said about both of them.

He touched the front of his shoulders with both hands, and then drew his hands forward into fists facing his body.

Frog wrote the last word of her letter: *strong.*

Two bright yellow leaves fell off the branch above them and twirled in tandem side by side. Frog caught one leaf before it hit the ground. And Charlie caught the other.

Acknowledgments

Thank you to my editor, Tracey Keevan—it's been such a joy working with you. I've learned so much from our collaboration. Thank you also to Esther Cajahuaringa, Marci Senders, Dan Kaufman, Amy Goppert, Sara Liebling, Guy Cunningham, Jody Corbett, Chip Poakeart, Dina Sherman, Kelly Jean Clair, Allison Grow, Jose Sabatini, and everyone at Disney Hyperion who has been so helpful in this journey. Thank you to my agent, Jennifer Carlson, for finding a home for my books with these wonderful people.

Carlisle Robinson *(carlisle-robinson.com)*, thank you for bringing Charlie and Frog to life through your artwork.

Thank you to Beth Bacon, Derrick Behm, Meghan Blackmon, Patrick Hulse, Leslie Hussey, Joshua Josa, Jackie Lightfoot, Glenn Lockhart, Diana Sea Markel, Carol McAfee, Kelsey Mitchell, Karen Levy Newnam, Diana Walsh O'Toole, and Vivienne Schroeder. Your feedback, comments, and insights were invaluable.

Thank you to Vivienne Schroeder for the story behind Charlie's name sign, Glenn Lockhart for naming the Flying Hands Café, Janis Cole for answering my ASL questions, Janice and Bill Adams for our discussion about DeafBlind communication, Jason Cacioppo for information on time-lapse cameras, and Eaddy Holmes,

Lucy Risher, and Iris V. Russell for their help with my sign descriptions.

Thank you to Diana and Shawn O'Toole for my Colorado visit and book tour, and to Lori Ann Johnson and Vicki Bond for making my visit to Arizona a successful one. Thank you to my great-niece Riley Mooney for coming all the way from Virginia Beach for my book launch party.

Hayley, thank you for your help with my website and social media. Isa, thank you for being one of my readers. I love you both, my strong, smart, kind daughters.

David, thank you for your editorial eye and for the myriad ways you support me and my writing. Your experience finding language and friendship in the Deaf community enriched and deepened this book. I love you.

Finally, thank you to the people within these communities who make up *my* community: the Washington, DC, and Gallaudet Deaf and interpreting communities, Vermont College of Fine Arts community, my classmates the Inkredibles, the Past Tense Yoga community, my Monroe Street neighbors, and, last but never least, my family and friends near and far. You mean more to me than you can possibly know.

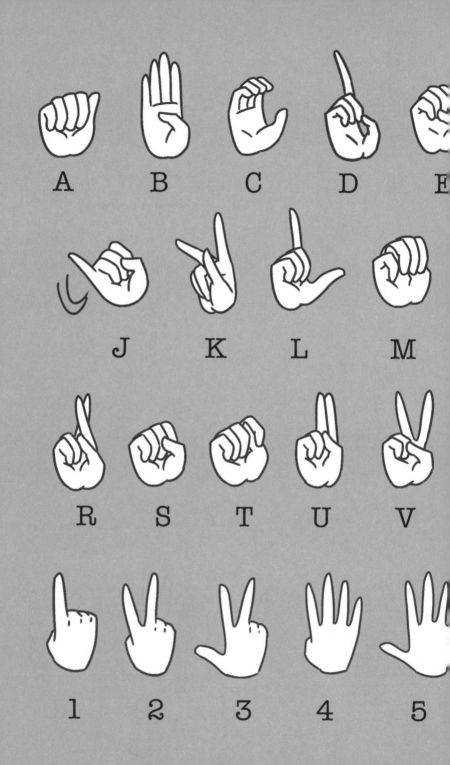